D0330820

THE 12 DARES OF CHRISTA

Also by Marissa Burt

Storybound
Story's End
A Sliver of Stardust
A Legend of Starfire

THE
12 DARES
OF
CHRISTA

MARISSA BURT

KATHERINE TEGEN BOOKS
An Imprint of HarperCollins Publishers

Katherine Tegen Books is an imprint of HarperCollins Publishers.

The 12 Dares of Christa

ISBN 978-0-06-241618-6
Typography by Aurora Parlagreco
17 18 19 20 21   CG/LSCH   10 9 8 7 6 5 4 3 2 1

❖

First Edition

For anyone longing for home

1

"POUR THE EGGNOG," I SAY as I come down the stairs late in the afternoon. "I've finished the list, and you both better prepare yourselves."

"Prepare ourselves?" Mom looks up from the sofa, where she's reading through her latest script.

"I don't think we have eggnog." Dad's voice comes from inside the open refrigerator, followed by the sound of cartons being rearranged on the shelves.

"Don't even play." I flop my stack of papers down on the kitchen table with a thump. "I know it's in there."

"Pumpkin eggnog." Dad pops his head out from the fridge, studying the jug of deliciousness. "I didn't even know they made pumpkin eggnog."

"They make pumpkin everything." I pull three glasses

down from the cabinet. "It is, after all, November first."

"Is it?" Mom says in a distracted voice. "It's warm for November."

"Yeah," Dad says thoughtfully. "And we haven't even had a real snowstorm yet."

"Come *on*, you guys. Have you forgotten? *November first?*" I wonder if they're just giving me a hard time. No way they don't remember that the first day of November is when we set the Best Christmas Plan Ever into motion. I glance back and forth between them, but Mom's immersed in her play, and Dad stares at me blankly for just a second too long. Then he visibly jolts.

"Of course! November first!" He hands me the unopened carton and laughs sheepishly. "I guess with how busy it's been and Halloween and everything, you know, I kind of forgot."

"Very funny, Dad." I wave the papers I'm holding at him. "I pulled out our plans from last year and tweaked them a little so we can have all our Chicago Christmas fun early, since, you know, we'll be in EUROPE on CHRISTMAS DAY!" I can never talk about that part without shouting, because, well, EUROPE!

"Great idea! We really should hammer out some of the details." Mom tosses her script onto the ottoman and joins us in the kitchen. "Your dad and I wanted to have a family powwow tonight anyway." She gives Dad a funny look. "Maybe we should order pizza first."

"Ooooh, yes! We'll need fortification." I pour the eggnog for everyone. "Make it an extra-large Pizza Surprise, okay?"

"Are you sure?" Dad gives me a weak laugh and reaches for his phone. "Last time the surprise was olives and pickles."'

"C'mon, Dad," I say. "Live a little. And while we're waiting for the delivery guy to get here, I can show you the Best Christmas Plan Ever for this year."

"I might need something stronger to go with this eggnog," Mom mutters under her breath, and reaches for the coffeepot.

"I heard that!" I settle in at the table and wait for them to join me.

"Okay," Dad says once the order is placed. He turns to Mom. "Do you—?" he begins, but Mom shakes her head slightly and grips her mug of steaming coffee even tighter.

"Let's have Christa show us what she's been working on first. Then we can talk."

I ignore how weird they're being, because we have more important things to get settled. Like Christmas plans. "Right. So it's basically the stuff we do every year." I hand out the pages I've been fiddling with all afternoon.

I spent the most time on the little sketches I've drawn in charcoal across the top of each page: a gingerbread house, reindeer pulling a sleigh, and a giant Christmas tree. "I just bumped it all up a few weeks so that we can make sure we don't miss anything." I run my finger down the list. "Our big Black Friday campout will be the day after Thanksgiving, obviously, and then the first two weeks in December we'll need to squeeze in the decorating, putting up the tree, making cookies, more shopping, ice-skating . . ." I trail off once I see that Mom and Dad aren't reading along. Instead, they're looking intently at me. Again with the weirdness. I drop my sheet. "What? What did I say?"

Mom's eyes grow all watery and Dad stares down at his hands.

"Christa," Dad finally says really slowly. "Christmas is going to be different this year."

"Oh, I totally get that!" I say, a wave of relief flooding me. Is *that* what they're worried about? That I'm going to be bummed about spending Christmas in Europe? Um, not likely. "I just figured we could do all the new Europe stuff *and* our usual traditions, too. I mean, I know none of the plans are guarantees. Mom may be super busy with her play performances when we're in Europe or we might not be able to get a tree put up in the hotel or—"

Dad clears his throat. This time, there's no mistaking the weirdness. He's starting to cry, too.

I drop my papers and lean back in my chair. "What? What is it?"

"Christa, we have something we need to tell you." Mom says it like she's doing the voice-over for a sad moment in one of her commercials. Except it's not an acting scene; it's my life. "We're getting a divorce."

I feel like I did the day in PE when Travis Rogers threw a ball right at me and I didn't dodge quickly enough. All my breath is gone, and I literally might barf all over the table.

Before anyone can say anything else, the doorbell rings, and Dad reaches for his wallet. "I guess I'd better get that."

"Leave it, Adam," Mom says without looking away from my face.

It's quiet for a minute, and then Dad clears his throat. "We've been thinking a long time about this, really trying to work it out, but we've come to the realization that we just aren't compatible anymore."

I stare at Dad. His words are English, but it's like I still need a translator. What does he mean? How can a family just stop *being compatible* with one another?

The doorbell rings again, more insistently this time, and Dad gets to his feet. "Hold that thought."

Mom jumps in while Dad is gone. "We want things to be good—for all of us. We want to be done with the fighting." She gives a shaky laugh. "We really always were better friends than anything."

I'm hearing her words, but they aren't computing. *How is this possible?* For *my* parents? I know kids whose parents are divorced. Heck, half of my class has some kind of quirky stepfamily thing going on, but seriously? *My* parents? The ones who used to dance together in the kitchen like some cheesy couple out of a movie? The ones who laugh at all the same stupid cat memes? The ones who went to Florence a couple of years ago for their fifteen-year anniversary?

Mom is saying more, something about growing and becoming different people and wanting different things.

"Different things?" I manage, and my voice comes out all choked. I realize I'm crying, the hot tears unstoppable. "You don't want our family anymore?" I don't believe this. How can they not want us to be together?

"Aw, honey," Mom says, and her voice cracks. She unclasps her fingers and reaches for mine, but my hand sits like a frozen lump under hers. "Of course we want our family. We love you so much, Christa." She glances over at Dad, who is standing in the doorway. "Both of us do, and whatever else changes, that will always be the same."

"It's really important that you hear us say that." Dad sets the pizza box down and slides into the chair closest to me. "And that you hear that it's not your fault. Our decision is because of us, not you. We tried to make it work, but really, we feel that this divorce will be the best thing for our family."

My body is catching up with my brain. Not my fault? What is *that* supposed to mean? The blood rushes to my flushed cheeks, and I can tell my heart is pounding fast. The speechless shock has turned into a hard knot of anger. I want to tell them to shut up. To shout at them that they can't mean what they're saying. If they loved me, they wouldn't be doing this! If they cared about us, they wouldn't break us apart! There's no way splitting up our family is *best* for our family, but I can't make myself say anything, because trying to stop crying has turned into ugly hiccups.

"Why?" I force the words out. "I don't"—*hiccup*—"understand. *Why* don't you want to be together"—*hiccup*—"anymore?"

Dad sighs and opens his mouth, but Mom interrupts.

"Let me answer." She turns to me. "It's something that's been coming on for a long time. I don't want you to worry about the details—that's too much of a load to put on a kid's shoulders. Believe me, I know." She's told me before how Gramps and Grams divorced when she was a teenager, how hard it was. Which is another reason I never thought it would happen to my parents.

Mom licks her lips and takes a deep breath. "You just have to trust us that we're doing what we think is best."

Mom didn't answer my question. I reach for my egg-nog, trying to gulp away the huge lump in my throat. I want to run upstairs to my room, grab my old ratty teddy bear, and tunnel under the covers before the sobs escape, but I know Mom and Dad will just follow me up there, and I really might explode if I have to look into their super-concerned faces anymore. Besides, sobbing with a teddy bear is *so* not how thirteen-year-olds are supposed to respond to news like this. I mean, I'm old enough to get the fact that people break up sometimes, and I'm totally old enough to notice that things haven't exactly been wonderful around here lately. Something clicks into place.

"Wait. What about Europe? What about Christmas?" My hiccups are gone. Even to me, my voice sounds hard.

Dad exchanges a look with Mom. "You guys are going

to get some mother-daughter time together in Europe," he says in a fake cheerful voice.

"You're not coming?" I shove my seat away from Dad's and stand up, knocking over my glass in the process. I glare at Mom. "Seriously? You're going to make him stay here?"

"*We*," Dad says, emphasizing the *we*, "think it might be helpful to do something different this year, especially for the holidays."

I don't want to listen to them anymore. I don't want to think about what they're saying. I stare down at my ruined plans, the pages now covered in a thick layer of eggnog, but they're blurring with more tears, and I feel about four years old and really wish I could go get a hug from them, but it's *them* who are the problem this time. "How long have you known?"

They don't answer that question either. "It's okay to feel angry, Christa," Dad says, hunching his shoulders over the table as though he can draw near me with his words.

"How long?" I ask.

"Since August," Mom says.

August. Three months ago.

"We decided in August," Dad says, "but we only signed the divorce papers yesterday."

He says it like that somehow makes it better.

"We didn't want to tell you right before the school year started. We thought the holidays could be sort of a transition."

They are saying more, something about always being friends, about it being mutual and how we can all make it work, but I'm still stuck on *divorce papers. Divorce. Divorce. Divorce.* It's like my brain is replaying it over and over so it can sink in.

"Chris?" Mom asks, her voice pitched slightly higher. "Are you okay, honey? Say something."

"Don't push her," Dad says, his voice tight.

Mom gets all stiff and begins to pick at her napkin, shredding its edges into little balls of paper.

"A transition to what?" I ask in a wooden voice. My friend Kari's parents live in the same neighborhood, so she can just flop back and forth whenever, but Emily's family isn't like that. Her dad only sees her on holidays. And then there is my BFF, Dani, who has about fifty thousand Thanksgiving dinners to attend because of all the step-relations. I get that divorce is kind of normal. After all, Kari and Emily and Dani are totally fine. I just never thought it would happen to me.

But it is happening. Like, for real. Mom and Dad have

it all planned. They lay out the details, and it seems every sentence is peppered with the word *divorce*. After the divorce, Mom's going to sign a lease on a new apartment in the Loop so she can be closer to the theater district. The divorce lawyer suggested that Dad keep the town house. I'll live with Dad during the week, so even after the divorce, I'll be able to stay at the same school, and then I'll go into the city on the weekends and school breaks to be with Mom. *Divorce. Divorce. Divorce.* You know how sometimes you can say a word over and over and after a while it starts to lose its meaning? Well, not so much with *divorce*. No matter how many times I hear *divorce*, the meaning stays the same, because that word changes everything.

2

Five weeks later

IT'S MIDMORNING WHEN DAD DRIVES me to the airport. He has the radio set to NPR, where mellow voices announce the local Christmas tree lightings, which, of course, I'm missing out on this year. Instead of the Best Christmas Plan Ever, the past few weeks have been filled with the Worst Divorce Preparations Ever. Moving Mom out, getting my new room set up, watching Mom and Dad awkwardly try to divide up a hundred everyday things in the town house until Mom finally said, "Forget it! I'll just go shopping." Yeah, it stank. Between that and scrambling around to get ready for the Europe trip, the past few weeks haven't exactly been very merry.

I glare at the radio dial as if that will make them stop talking about all the fun Chicago Christmas things that will happen without me. The digital display reads 11:01, which is super weird. Those are my least favorite numbers ever since November first became the day I found out about the divorce. I hope it isn't an omen or something. Today of all days; today, when I'm about to fly halfway around the world; today, when I'm leaving Dad to go on tour with Mom; today, when I wish I could go home and climb back into bed and wake up again and have everything magically return to the way it was last year; today those are not good numbers to see. I take a deep breath and stare at the dashboard until it switches to 11:02.

Dad takes a sip from his travel mug, and the familiar smell of coffee plus his favorite hazelnut creamer drifts toward me. Good old Dad, driving his same old beat-up pickup, wearing the same tattered overcoat he's had forever, drinking from the same photo travel mug I got him for Father's Day two years ago. The pictures on it show all three of us playing in the surf at the beach one summer, sailing little paper boats in the fountain downtown, sitting in front of the flocked Christmas tree I begged us to get a few years ago, but the colors are all faded now.

I feel that lump in my throat again, the one that appears whenever I think how different everything is going to be this year. No Christmas at home. No flocked tree, no ice-skating downtown, no last-minute Christmas shopping, no Christmas party with my friends, no caroling, no cookie making, no Most Wonderful Time of the Year.

I try to shut those thoughts off. I mean, come *on*. Europe! I should be dying to go. And I totally would be if we had gone on this trip, say, seven months ago. With *both* Mom and Dad. And *not* at Christmastime. Because as awesome as Europe is, nothing, and I mean nothing, beats Christmas. Okay, so I know there's Christmas in Europe, but it's not the same. Like everything else in my life, Christmas is going to be really different this year.

"Chris," Dad says over the NPR news briefing. "You haven't even touched the doughnuts. Come on. Dig in. You don't want to count on the airplane food being actually edible."

I reach for the red-and-green bag that's perched on the seat behind Dad and unroll it to scope out the options. Two maple doughnuts—one with some kind of crunchy cereal on it and another with a mystery topping—a fancy one with silver snowmen on wintry white frosting, and a couple of unidentifiable filled doughnuts. *Shoot.*

"Hand me a maple bar," Dad says. I oblige and can feel his sideways gaze on me. "Don't you want to try one of the others? The lady at the shop said they're the newest flavors."

I shake my head and start to fold the bag back up. No way do I want to try some sort of surprise doughnut on the way to a transatlantic flight.

"There's another layer under there," Dad says around a mouthful of doughnut. "Old-fashioned glazed."

I ignore the tight knot of guilt. "Old-fashioned doughnuts are classic," I say, unearthing one and taking a perfect bite with a sigh. No fancy sprinkles or trendy flavors or layers of weird crunchy toppings. Flying halfway around the globe is wild enough; I don't need what I put in my mouth to be some kind of new experience, *thankyouverymuch*.

Outside the car window, soft flakes drift down, coating everything with a thin white layer. "I wonder if it will snow anywhere in Europe," I say as I pull out the water bottle tucked into my backpack and take a sip.

"Probably not in London," Dad says. "And it's not likely in Florence either, though parts of Italy get snow. There's a slight possibility it might in Paris." Dad owns a travel agency, so he knows all about travel and other countries, but I hope he's wrong. Christmas just wouldn't feel right without snow.

I reach for the second old-fashioned doughnut in the bag, making sure not to touch the mystery one next to it.

"Old-fashioned *again*?" Dad clears his throat. "I'm looking forward to hearing what you think about all the different European delicacies. I hope you'll try all sorts of new things. You'll be visiting some of the most famous food locales in the world. What an adventure!" Dad always talks about travel as "an adventure." His job, after all, is to help people plan their dream trips around the world, so he has some pretty incredible stories about visiting the Great Wall and the Taj Mahal and a million other exotic places. But his voice sounds a little too cheerful.

I stare at the doughnut. I hate it that Dad has started commenting on what I eat. I mean, I really, really hate it. Believe me, I'd love it if I could go back to the way it used to be, if I could grab the mystery doughnut and go for it, just like old Christa. But I can't. Like, literally can't.

"I guess," I say, and try to spin my new food preferences as a joke or a quirk or something. "Don't judge. Classics are classic for a reason. If you want to be all crazy with your food while I'm gone, have fun with that. I'm just glad Europe is also famous for its bread."

Dad laughs, and I can tell he's trying to be playful, too. "Trying something new won't kill you, you know."

Um, I have to disagree. Last month, a girl at my school accidentally ate a cookie with some peanuts in it and nearly died. The nurse had to inject her with a shot and everything, and then she was rushed to the ER. She was okay, but seriously, food *could* have killed her. After that, I learned from WebMD that food allergies can strike at any age. I know, I know, no one should ever read WebMD, but I did, okay, and it was useful and might save my life someday, because there is no way that I'm buying this whole "try it, it won't kill you" line that people are always saying. I would like to *live, thankyouverymuch*, so old-fashioned doughnuts and plain water it is. Besides. Surprises are overrated.

Now the quiet in the car feels anything but sleepy. I'm going to have to try to fill up the silence so Dad doesn't start thinking more about what I eat. Or don't eat.

"What I want to know is what you're going to do on Christmas Day without me." I grab a napkin and wipe the sugar glaze off my fingers. "I guess you can watch the movie marathon on your own, and we've already put up the tree, but how in the world will you do the Great Vasile Scavenger Hunt solo? The neighbors are going to think you're nuts!"

Every year Dad plans a scavenger hunt for me and my friends by setting it up with all the neighbors ahead of time. Sometimes it's simple, like snapping a photo of as many ornaments as you can, and there are prizes for the wackiest one, the sweetest one, the silliest one, that sort of thing. It's so corny. But also a lot of fun, because our neighbors are great and they always also give us loads of candy. One year my friends and I had to look for tacky Christmas sweaters. Another, different kinds of wrapping paper. Last year it was shapes of Christmas cookies.

"Did you ever find all the different cookies last year?" Dad asks. He had wanted to pair it up with caroling, so after we sang—ridiculously off-key for everyone but my best friend, Dani—the neighbors had trays of cookies for us to choose from.

"All but an elf," I tell him. "Who makes elf cookies, anyway? That's like cannibalism or something."

Dad laughs. "I'll make sure to bake a whole batch of elf cookies while you're gone. That way I can think of you whenever I turn cannibal and eat them."

The pristine layer of snow has melted into ugly slush by the time we get off the highway for the O'Hare exit. I see it slumped up on the side of the road in depressing dirty clumps. It matches the gray of the asphalt and the darker gray of the leafless trees against the gray clouded sky. Gray, gray, gray. *Bah.* We drive up to the toll booth, and Dad puts down his window to toss the change inside, letting in a gust of frigid air. I sink deeper into my new coat. Bright yellow felt to combat the grayness of the winter.

"Now, Chris," Dad says, warmth returning to the car

as he puts the window back up and we accelerate. "Don't forget to enjoy this trip to the fullest. Anyone's first visit to Europe is formative. Your whole outlook may be changed after two weeks in the Old Country."

"I know, I know," I say. I've heard him give his travel company spiel a thousand times before. "It's going to be unforgettable and fabulous and worth every penny." I try to tell my groggy and gray almost-homesick self that I am headed to Europe. *Europe!* But I'm not sure it works, and I wonder if I still will have to go if somehow there's a miraculous 11:30 a.m. weekend airport traffic jam and I miss my flight.

The car is slowing down now, pulling in toward the departures drop-off. While we wait for a space to open up, Dad turns toward me. "Don't forget that I love you. I know you are going to have a grand adventure. Just promise me one thing."

"O-kay." I really don't want to have some gushy farewell scene at the airport.

Dad pulls up to the curb and lets the car idle. "Promise me that you'll allow the unexpected to lead you someplace you were always meant to go."

"Um." I let out a half laugh that helps keep me from actually starting to cry and look at Dad to see if he's teasing.

What is that supposed to mean? Next he'll tell me I should "follow my dreams" and "be true to myself" or something. "Is that from your new travel brochure or what?"

"Maybe." Dad grins. "But I mean it. I know the past few weeks have been difficult, Chris, and maybe some things have changed that you wished could stay the same."

I look down at the charm bracelet on my wrist, the one Dad gave me when I first learned about the trip, and study the miniature Eiffel Tower, Big Ben, and the famous bridge in Florence—all things I'm going to be seeing in the next few days. I know he's talking about the divorce.

"But change doesn't have to be bad," Dad continues. "Give the unexpected a chance. Let Europe awaken that part of you, the part that I know loves surprises and challenges, and fantastic things might happen. I love you, honey."

"I love you, too, Dad." I lean over to give him a half hug. "I'll miss you." Oh, man! I *am* going to cry.

"Your mom's over there, waiting by the curbside check-in," he says. "Go on now. You want plenty of time to get to the international terminal."

I get my backpack while Dad pops the trunk, coming around with my new luggage. The big suitcase is plain black but my carry-on has the cutest little dog silhouettes printed all over it. I've never needed real rolling luggage before now, so Dad took me to pick it out last week. And for some reason, thinking about that makes me want to cry even more.

Dad attaches them to each other. "Don't forget about the time change. I'm seven hours behind you in Florence and Paris. Six in London. Think of that before you text me in the middle of the night to tell me all about your adventures. Have fun, sweetie."

I give him one final hug and then roll my bags over to the kiosk where Mom is waiting. I know Dad's right. This is a big adventure, and it's supposed to be awesome, and it probably will be. I get all of that, I really do. But there's this part of me that seriously can't believe my dad isn't coming along, too. And an even bigger part of me, the part that sees my dad sitting alone on his side of the table in the morning or watches Mom trade out the big coffee-pot for a little single-serve one, wonders if it wouldn't be worth skipping Europe altogether if we could just have a normal, quiet Christmas all together at home.

3

"CHRISTA! OVER HERE!" MOM SAYS from behind her big dark sunglasses. "Wait. We have to do this the European way." She sets down the two coffee cups she's holding and grabs my shoulders, kissing the air on either side of my cheeks. "You look marvelous in that coat, Chris. And I love your new luggage. Very cosmopolitan. Ready for world travel."

"Hi, Mom," I say. Maybe it's clichéd for an actress, but Mom always wears black with a single tiny pop of color. Today, she's got on a black sweater and leggings with a woolen wrap that matches her boots, and her dark hair is pulled back with a bright red scarf. Even the way she moves is dramatic.

Everyone is always saying how similar Mom and I are,

but I think that's just because we look alike. We both are on the short side, with dark eyes that crinkle up in the corners, long straight noses, impossible-to-manage crazy-thick hair, and the same coppery skin tone. In my opinion, that's where the similarities end.

"Here. Hot chocolate. Your favorite." Mom hands me the cup with a flourish.

"Thanks." I follow her toward the attendant who is express checking in our bags.

"Now," Mom says. "I've got a bunch of travel guides in my carry-on, and a fat stack of old issues of *People* so we can have a big trashy magazine binge on the plane. I hope you brought prepackaged snacks. International flights have the worst food. Or we can get something to take on once we pass through security." Mom doesn't need a reminder about having an adventure. Going to the grocery story with her is an adventure, because she has no neutral—she lives in either high gear or exhausted mode. Today, she's 100 percent energy, and just being around her makes everything seem more awake and alive.

While we stand in the long security line, Mom chats with the family behind us, who are headed to the West Coast. "LA is fabulous," Mom says. "You are going to *love* it. Especially this time of year." It is classic Mom to make friends wherever she goes.

I take a sip of my cocoa and immediately remove the lid. *Cinnamon.* The barista has sprinkled spices and some chewy things all over the whipped cream. Definitely not on my known foods list. I mean, I know spontaneous anaphylaxis—which is what happens when your body suddenly becomes deathly allergic to something—is super rare, but it *does* happen to some people. And exactly what am I supposed to do if I'm on a transatlantic flight with an anaphylaxis problem from these stupid mysterious chewy things? My heart starts to beat faster. My throat feels a little tight—is it starting to swell up? I check out my skin for evidence of hives. Clear so far. My stomach twists as I look at the treacherous cup of cocoa.

It totally sucks to be afraid of new foods. Really, it sucks to be afraid at all. Don't even get me started on the whole plane flight thing. I've taken a few trips before. Small ones. But I haven't flown since last year, and now all I can think about is how freakin' crazytown it is that we pile onto this metal tube and fly through the air insanely fast thousands of feet above the ground and act like it's normal.

Deep breaths, Chris. Take deep breaths. The security guy says I have to finish the drink or toss it before he lets me through, so I happily chuck it in the trash. The internet told me that most allergic reactions happen within thirty minutes of consuming something, so at least I'll have the moment of truth before we board the plane.

Once we're at the gate, Mom plops her carry-on and purse down near the window. "I'm going to see if we can upgrade to business class. Wish me luck."

"Good luck," I say, pulling out my phone to distract me from the aftertaste of cinnamon. Is my mouth a little itchy? Or is that just normal? I keep taking deep breaths as I skim through my latest photos. Dani and me in front of Buckingham Fountain. Me eating a huge slice of pizza with a long string of cheese stretching between the piece and my mouth. Dad making a silly face while signing his name on the wall of a restaurant. The three of us with the corner fiddler at the Christkindlmarket.

I try to find the excited-for-something-new part of me so she can give the rest of me a pep talk. *Europe! This is amazing!* I'm getting out of school a whole two weeks early! I'm about to have an adventure! But it doesn't work. The spontaneous part of me is huddled in the corner right now, trying not to freak out about cinnamon. I sigh, slipping my phone back in my pocket.

"All set," Mom says, a wave of her spicy perfume announcing her return. "We've got exit-row seats in business class." Mom squeals. "Does it get any better than that?" She perches next to me and pulls out three fat guidebooks. "Florence, Paris, and London. I can hardly believe it! I haven't been to Europe in years, and here we are going together!" Little pink and lavender heart-shaped Post-its are sticking out of the books like quills on a porcupine. "I've marked a whole bunch of things—way more than we can ever see—but planning is half the fun, isn't it? Besides, why do when you can overdo?"

I can't help but laugh. Overdoing is kind of Mom's thing. I pick up the book for Florence, which is our first stop. I've seen these guides in Dad's office before, without all the girly Post-its, of course.

Mom thumbs through the Paris guide. "Just think of the shopping! And look! The famous theater from *The Phantom of the Opera*." Mom folds the book back on its cover, creasing it wide. "I can't believe we're actually doing this. My favorite daughter and I are off to Europe."

I roll my eyes. That joke is so old. "I'm your only daughter, Mom."

Mom picks up my hand and examines my fingernails, which I painted mini Christmas trees on last night. "Ooooh, I like." She pats my hand. "Have I told you how glad I am we're doing this?"

"Only a thousand times." Getting cast in a play that tours Europe has been one of Mom's lifelong dreams. And this is the year it's finally coming true. I wonder if there's any part of Mom that's a teensy bit sad things have worked out this way. That her big year for touring Europe was the same year she and Dad split up. What would it have been like to do this when the three of us were still together as a family? I guess I'll never know, because now it's just me and Mom and an empty seat next to us where Dad should be.

I know, I know, they're divorced. It happened. End of story. I'm not some five-year-old who hopes her parents are going to get back together. Well, not really, though it wouldn't be awful if they somehow did, right? Anyway, things are different now. I get that. But it sucks when things change whether you want them to or not, you know? I stare at the page in front of me, which shows a sunset picture of the Florence skyline.

"Does it really look like this?" I ask Mom.

"Better," Mom says with a grin.

Just then someone comes up behind us, standing in that too-close-for-strangers zone.

"Oh! Todd!" Mom says in an extra-cheerful voice, standing to hug the man who's appeared from nowhere.

"It's so good to see you!"

"Hey, Todd," I say, but with a whole lot less enthusiasm. Her fellow actor Todd has been featuring in Mom's conversations a lot lately, like, as maybe more than just friends. Unfortunately, unlike all the boyfriends for newly divorced parents in every movie I've ever seen, he's not mean or super flaky or hiding some secret agenda to steal the family fortune. Not that we have a family fortune, but still. The worst I can say of Todd is that he seems suspiciously like too much of a Mr. Nice Guy. But does Mom see that? Or does she think that Todd, with his too-perfect hair, and his too-perfect smile, and his movie-star good looks, is potential dating material?

"Not boarding yet, hmm?" Todd says, sliding into the empty seat across from us.

I set the guidebook aside as another realization hits me. I didn't really pay attention to all the casting details when Mom told me about the trip, but if Todd is here, it probably means that his daughter—

"CHRIS!" A too-chipper voice confirms my hunch. *"Ohmigosh!* I can't believe we're going to France, can you? And together?" She pulls me up from my seat in her excitement, and I have to work to keep my balance.

"Hey, Kylie," I say. Kylie Barrows. Gorgeous, over-the-top happy—like a chipmunk or a cheerleader might be—über-nice Kylie Barrows. Who really needs to drink decaf only. I spent two weeks last summer at camp with Kylie. We were cabinmates, not BFFs, like you'd think from the way she's welcoming me. It's not that Kylie is a Bad Person or anything. In fact, she, like her dad, is a super-nice one. But she comes in this mega-caffeinated package of trying-to-be-friends-with-everyone that I don't know what to do with. Being around her makes me feel instantly tired.

"It'ssogoodtoseeyou!" Kylie gushes, her greeting coming out as one long word squished together. She enfolds me in a hug and a cloud of fruity fragrance. I pat her on the back, awkwardly, her long, tight curls crunching under my hand.

"Aren'tyoujustsoexcited? I couldn't even sleep last night! Europe! We're going to Europe!" Kylie's pace slows as she divides her attention between me and whatever texting conversation she has going on in her phone.

"Totally. Super excited." With Kylie, sometimes it doesn't really matter what you say. She's going so fast that she just steamrolls right over your answers. She's monologuing about how they got stuck in traffic on the way to the airport, and I put in a few "Ohs" and "Reallys," but I'm actually focused on what is going on over her shoulder, where Todd is leaning in and smiling at Mom. Whatever he says makes Mom throw back her head and laugh. Then she flips her hair and readjusts the sunglasses on her forehead. Is Mom just being her usual exuberant self or is she actually . . . *flirting* with him? *Oh no.* Something totally *is* going on between the two of them. What if Todd is part of Mom's new "life direction," whatever that is supposed to mean?

The boarding area around us begins to fill up with other passengers. Kylie has moved on from the potential airplane turbulence to the pros and cons of French food—which, given that she's never been out of America, is an incredibly long list!—to scrolling through her phone's photo album, which is bursting with pics of her "sweet cat Freckles." I look helplessly toward Mom for rescue, but Mom is still zeroed in on Todd. This time, they have their theater scripts out, so I know they're talking about work. I'm on my own unless I want to hear Freckles's life story until it's time to board the plane.

"So, Kylie." I interrupt her midrecitation of the way Freckles likes to sit on her laptop keyboard. "Do you know which other kids are coming on the trip?" I point toward a trio of boys our age who are leaning up against the wall opposite. I think I recognize one of the adults near them as one of Mom's castmates. "What about those guys?"

"Ohmigosh, I hope so!" Kylie said. "That one guy on the end is so cute."

I scan the waiting area to see if there might be some girls our age, too, but I linger on the group of boys again. The one guy *is* kind of cute, in a hipster-geeky sort of way. He's a little taller than the other two, with curly brown hair that looks like he's forgotten to comb it, and a serious face. The boy next to Hipster has super-pale skin and bright red hair. He's wearing a T-shirt that reads "Weasley's Wizard Wheezes" and holding a tablet that they're all looking at.

"That's so wicked," Harry Potter Kid says, and then high-fives the third boy, who has short, spiky hair. Spiky Hair can't stop moving. Even while looking at the tablet, he's bouncing up and down on his tiptoes.

"Do you recognize anybody else?"

"Huh?" Kylie is only half listening, her thumbs working mind-bogglingly fast on her phone's touch pad.

"Never mind," I say as the flight attendant announces our boarding instructions, first in Italian, then French, then English. Mom appears after that, and it takes us what feels like forever to board the metal-tube-death-trap, I mean, the plane. One good part—okay, maybe the only good part of the boarding process—is that I discover there are twenty rows between us and Todd and Kylie, so that's one less thing to worry about for now. Mom's bulging carry-on barely fits overhead, and I pull out my earbuds so I can listen to my Christmas playlist. The internet tells me that most plane accidents happen during landing or takeoff, so you'd better believe that I'll be counting down until we're at cruising altitude.

A text bings on my phone, and I see that it's from Dad: **Don't forget! Allow the unexpected to lead you someplace you were always meant to go.** I try not to think about how in a plane the unexpected could mean *DEATH*. I pull out the plastic safety card from the side pocket and curl up against the cold window. I've read it all before online, but it's important to know what to do in case of an emergency.

"Oh, honey," Mom says when she catches me comparing the emergency exit door to the little cartoon diagram on the card. "Put that away." She snatches it out of my fingers and hands me a magazine instead. "Let's have some fun."

And Mom is fun. Between giggling at the ridiculous *What Not to Wear* pages and playing Mom's favorite people-watching game of trying to guess what everyone around us is thinking, the takeoff passes in a blink. Soon, the seat belt sign flicks off with a ding. I've made it through the first part. Not long after that, I hear the sound of the snack cart wheeling up behind us. A flight attendant is at the helm, cheerily offering little packets of snacks, and behind her is Hipster Boy. I figure he's had the bad luck to try to go to the bathroom behind the cart and is stuck waiting.

"Um," I say when they get to our row. "Apple juice, please." The flight attendant serves us with her fixed-on grin.

"Coffee," Mom groans. "Oh, you're an angel."

"Pretzels or cookies?" the lady asks us, and Hipster grins at me.

"Get both," he says, and I stupidly go mute. Like, as in, I'm too flustered to talk.

"Would you like both?" the flight attendant says with a tired smile, but I'm still watching Hipster.

"Um," I say, but my brain seems to be functioning in super slow motion. I feel weird with cute Hipster Boy watching me, like he'll be able to see inside me and discover that both pretzels and cookies with potential nut contamination terrify me. "Both would be great," Mom says to the flight attendant.

Hipster Boy continues on without a second glance, but I want to disappear under the seat with my flotation device.

Since when have I ever not been able to talk to someone, even a particularly cute someone? I watch the boy as he follows the cart up the aisle, laughing and joking with the flight attendants. I poke at the two unopened packages on my tray and then stuff them in the seat pocket in front of me, stifling a yawn. Despite the coffee, Mom has already nodded off, her head resting on my shoulder, eyes hidden by wide-lensed sunglasses.

I do not sleep at all during the flight. Instead, I watch the two Christmas movies I've uploaded onto my tablet—a kiddie one with puppies and stockings, and the classic *White Christmas*. I try—and fail—to nap. I eat the airline food that's crammed on my little foldout tray—well, I have some of the crackers and apples that came with the meal. No way am I going to risk unknown ingredients thirty thousand feet in the air. I drink four apple juices and two Cokes from the cart. I flip through the airline shopping magazine with its collections of weird items I can't imagine anyone actually buying. Okay, so the garden elves dressed up as reindeer would look perfect around our outdoor Christmas tree, but not for $250. I play games on my phone. And I take I don't know how many treks back to the gross, smelly bathroom just to stretch my legs. And finally, *finally*, we are landing in Florence. Fortunately, I'm too wired and too exhausted to be very scared about the landing. There's only so much fight-or-flight adrenaline one's body can produce at once.

Soon, we're standing hunched over our seats, wedged behind the antsy passengers who just can't wait to pop out into the aisle and get their bags down before the plane door is even open.

"Jet lag is the worst," Mom says, running her fingers through her rumpled hair. "You only feel a little tired now, but give it a few hours. The important thing is to stay awake until a reasonable bedtime." Her overstuffed roll-behind carry-on keeps snagging on the seats, and she yanks it forward forcefully. "Ugh. I should have packed a duffel."

Mom applies a coat of red lipstick before we disembark, which makes her instantly transform from exhausted Mom into normal Mom. I don't know what I look like, but I feel like I've been living in a desert, with the airplane's recycled air gluing my eyeballs open and keeping my hair all staticky. I feel really tired, and all I want to do is get to our hotel and have a power nap. Okay, maybe more than a nap. I could probably sleep all day. I yawn for the fifty millionth time.

"Remember," Mom says. "To fight jet lag, you have to stay awake."

I give her a death glare that she successfully ignores. After waiting in line for what seems like forever, we get to passport control and have to answer all their questions about where we'll be staying and for how long. Mom is her usual charming self, explaining all about the theater group and our itinerary, but the agent doesn't seem won over. She frowns at Mom and scowls at me as she stamps our passports.

When we arrive at the baggage claim, Todd finds us, delivering Mom a cup of coffee that he's gotten from the vending machine near the bathrooms. Kylie trails behind him, two bottles of Coke held precariously in her phone-free hand. "Isn't this the best?" she asks, handing me one and glancing up from her screen. "I'm just finishing up this text from Lonna, my BFF back home. She says to say hi."

"Thanks for the Coke. And, um, hi to Lonna?" I have no idea who Lonna is. "Isn't it, like, the middle of the night in Chicago?" I take a big gulp of Coke, hoping that the caffeine will kick in soon.

Kylie shrugs. "Lonna says she's going to live vicariously through me. I have to send her every single detail. Come here." She grabs my elbow, flips up her phone, and snaps a selfie. "*Ohmigosh*, we look awful!" she says upon examination, and then proceeds to post it online for everyone to see.

Kylie's only wrong about the *we* part of that statement. Her trendy clothes are somehow wrinkle free and her hair is still neat and tidy. But me? Not so much. My eyes are bloodshot, my hair is squished down flat in the back, and I can almost see the stale airport air radiating from my clothes.

"*Ohmigosh*, you were right," Kylie says, slipping her phone into her pocket. "Those guys *are* with our group."

Over near the luggage cart, Hipster Boy, Harry Potter Kid, and Spiky Hair have gathered together again. Spiky Hair is hopping on and off the moving luggage track, as though he might take a ride out to the loading platform.

"Do the spin!" Harry Potter Kid says, and Spiky Hair spins on one hand, leaping back and forth over the low dividing wall.

"Oooh," Kylie breathes. "That's cool."

I have to admit, it is pretty impressive. Spiky Hair looks like someone in the parkour clips I've seen, or a break-dancer or something. I wonder how long it takes before a grown-up notices and they get in trouble. Another girl our age is also watching them. Her Asian features blend stylishly with a pixie cut that has a bright aqua streak over one ear, and she is wearing funky rainbow shoes.

"Christa," Mom says, coming up behind me and Kylie.

"We have to go straight to our first rehearsal." The *we* suspiciously refers to her and Todd. Well, and the other actors, who have now gathered at one end of the baggage area. "You guys will be with the tour guides, who are handling the kid portion of the tour." She hands me a Post-it–marked stack of papers. "This is your itinerary. Your tour guide, Madison, is supposed to be amazing— she comes highly recommended from an agency—and her assistant, Miles, grew up traveling through Europe with his parents." She peers over the tops of her sunglasses at the two college-aged people standing near Nic, the play's director. "Hmm, that must be them."

Madison is over near the luggage claim looking importantly at a clipboard. She's wearing tailored pants and a cowl-neck sweater. Her short hair perfectly frames her smooth brown skin and large dark eyes, which widen as she ticks things off a checklist. Even from where I'm standing, I can see the color-coded highlighter markings on the itinerary. She definitely looks like she's in charge. Next to her, Miles is joking with Harry Potter Kid. Miles is taller than the other boys, and even though he's only wearing jeans and a zip-up sweater, he looks a lot older.

"Miles and Madison are great," Todd says. "Kylie was in a group tour with them when I had a show in New York.

They do a really good job of showing the kids the sights and making it an educational experience for them." Todd gives Mom a quick squeeze on the shoulders that turns into a mini-massage.

I have to work hard not to roll my eyes. I know that theater people are all touchy-feely, but could Todd *be* any more obvious?

Mom shrugs his hands off, looking at her watch. "Okay. Well, I've got to run. Sweetie, have fun on your first day, and I'll see you at the hotel tonight."

After Mom gives me a quick hug, she and Todd disappear with the other grown-ups, leaving me alone, standing next to Kylie, who is sending Lonna pictures of the baggage claim. I can't believe Lonna is pulling an all-nighter for that. I flip through the pages of the itinerary and can barely stifle a groan at the first page.

"We don't get to go to our hotel first?" I feel like crying, but my eyeballs are too dry to make tears. *City Bus Tour of Florence* is blocked off for the rest of the afternoon. I skim the list of locations we'll get to see today and feel a tiny flare of excitement somewhere under all the exhaustion. Seeing this stuff is going to be incredibly cool, but you'd better believe I'd rather have a shower and a nap first.

"City tours are so fun," Kylie says. "You get to see everything in one big swoop. And if we have an Italian guide telling us about all the spots, I bet he's super cute."

"Right," I say, willing myself not to say something snarky. I mean, I like Kylie and all, and I like cute boys, but if I have to witness her boy craziness for the whole trip, I might lose my mind. I fold up the itinerary pages with a sigh. It seems that every minute with Madison and Miles is planned out. This afternoon we'll be touring until just before dinner, when we all have to go to an opening-week cast party. My visions of a long shower and a nap in my four-star hotel suite disappear in a puff of smoke as I see Madison headed our way.

4

"YOU TWO MUST BE CHRISTA and Kylie." Madison stands, her clipboard at the ready, with a smile that reveals perfectly whitened teeth. "I have a lot of terrific things planned for you all, and I promise you that you're going to have a fabulous trip." She waves behind her and beckons over the aqua-haired girl. "This is Sasha. Sasha, meet Kylie and Christa."

"Ohmigosh, Sasha! It's so nice to meet you!" Kylie squeals and gives Sasha a big hug. "Another girl! Three boys, three girls. It's perfect!"

I inwardly cringe and give Sasha a sympathetic smile.

"Hey," Sasha says, and gives me a nod once Kylie lets her go.

Madison checks the stopwatch hanging around her

neck. "Oops! We're four minutes late. Better get started!" Madison claps her hands together and pilots us over toward Miles, who is chilling with the boys. Harry Potter Kid and Spiky Hair are still playing with the baggage claim cart. Next to them, I can see Hipster Boy crouched over some color-coded maps of Florence. So he *is* definitely a part of this trip.

"We've got to go through customs now," Madison tells us. "This way. Stay on task, everyone." Madison bosses us all the way through the "nothing to declare" line, past the agent who stamps our customs card, and out into the lobby, where she finishes by ordering us to put our luggage in one pile. "Miles," she says. "Get a cart."

With a half smile, Miles obeys and starts loading everything onto a metal luggage cart.

"Okay, everybody," Madison says, drawing Hipster Boy and the other two boys into our circle, "in just a few minutes we'll be boarding Florence's excellent hop-on, hop-off sightseeing tour. The bus will take us by all the famous sights of this beautiful ancient city. We'll have lots of stops along the way where we can do a little exploring. And I have some great icebreakers planned so we can get to know one other." She glances up expectantly, as if we all should cheer at this or something. I feel like crawling into my suitcase and hiding. Icebreakers are practically a form of torture. Why do adults think playing awkward games with people you barely know is a fun thing to do?

"We're loaded up," Miles says, pushing the cart toward the double doors and the waiting tour bus outside. "Let's go."

Madison opens and closes her mouth, then purses her lips as if Miles is derailing her plan, but she follows after him anyway, herding us toward the minibus, where a pretty Italian woman stands at the front with a microphone.

"*Buongiorno*," the woman says in her exotic-sounding accent to each of us as we climb aboard. "Welcome to Italy. I am Luiza, and this is our driver, Antonio." Antonio is a sturdy-looking old man who tips his felt cap to us.

I collapse into a window seat. The bus is big enough that we should each be able to have our own row, which is a total bonus seeing how we've all flown overnight and no one has showered, but I have a sneaking suspicion that Kylie might not see it that way, so I pull my carry-on up next to me. Fortunately, Kylie sits with Sasha near the front, and the boys file into other spots.

The bus starts moving, and Luiza's melodic voice launches into an explanation of the history of Florence. The landscape around us stretches toward the hazy hills in the distance. The brilliant blue December sky contrasts with the faded green of winter fields. We pass low-lying houses with reddish roofs, and the buildings get closer together as we near the city center. I watch with interest as the countryside rolls by. Already, Italy feels so different from America. But barely fifteen minutes pass before I'm struggling to keep my eyes open. It's not that Luiza isn't saying interesting things or that the scenery isn't gorgeous. It's that my stupid eyelids are so heavy that I can barely keep them open. My head keeps dropping over to the window, where the buzz of the bus's motion lulls me to sleep. I prop my head up with my backpack, hoping that my first glimpses of European soil will help me stay awake. But it's no use; sleep wins, and I find myself closing my eyes and succumbing to a restless nap until Madison's authoritative voice wakes me to announce that we're at our first stop.

The Piazza del Duomo is one of the most famous sites in Florence. A huge open square connects several magnificent old buildings. Madison is telling us details about them, but my attention is caught by the breathtaking Christmas tree that fronts the first structure. It's decorated with gold and silver ornaments and red garland. I can only imagine how spectacular it will look at night. We pass by a life-size nativity with a tall wooden Mary and Joseph peering piously down at Baby Jesus before gathering in front of the octagon-shaped Baptistery, which has symmetrical windows and arches dotting its surface. I barely get a look at the famous paneled bronze doors before Madison claps her hands and calls us all together.

"Icebreaker number one!" she says, ticking something off her list. "We have a few minutes before it's our turn inside the cathedral."

I wish I were still asleep and only dreaming when I hear what she has planned for us. Why do grown-ups, even partial grown-ups like Madison, make kids do things that grown-ups would never do in a million years? By the time Madison is finished bossing us around, we're all standing on the steps outside the ancient bronze doors reaching across our circle to hold hands with one another. Then we're supposed to untwist and figure out how to get free. It's stupid. Here we are in an amazing old city with a million interesting things to see (or sleep through), and we are playing Human Knot, or whatever.

I end up with Kylie's hand in one of my mine and Spiky Hair's sweaty palm in another. We twist and turn, so that first I find myself outside of the group, hands stretched wide around the inner knot, and then tangled up inside, squished between Sasha and Hipster Boy. This is beyond stupid. And embarrassing. I mean, we don't even know everyone's names yet.

Finally, when we are almost untangled, Miles rescues us. "We're going to miss the tour," he says, pointing at his watch. "We need to wrap this up."

"Oh, right! Finish up, everybody!" Madison says. "It's time for us to go inside." Behind her, I see that some other tourists have been taking pictures of our human knot. Awesome. *We* have become a sight to see. I'm just glad they can't tag me when they post their photos online. Thankfully, once we're inside the cathedral, there is no more talk of icebreakers. Our guide explains how the bronze doors have carved panels that depict events from the life of Jesus Christ and other Bible stories. Even though I don't know most of the stories, the scenes are unbelievably lifelike and intricate, all the way down to the beards on the men's faces.

I've never worked with any kind of metal, but I do love sketching and painting. Or at least I used to. Seeing all of this brilliant art has me wishing I had at least packed my old sketchbook. Inside the cathedral, the floors are covered with shards of marble arranged into detailed geometric patterns, and the thick walls surround us with a quiet that's made even more noticeable by the muffled sounds of car horns and street noises outside. Sturdy-looking columns divide the cathedral into shadowy spaces. Green-and-white marble walls stretch up to a domed ceiling covered with a mosaic depicting religious scenes of angels and holy-looking people.

We linger in an alcove where a crèche exhibit is set up with nativities from different cultures lining the old stone walls. Last year I went to the crèche festival at Dani's church, and I loved seeing how artists depict the one famous scene. Here, there's a clay Baby Jesus wrapped up papoose-style next to his Native American mother. A blown-glass Asian Mary and Joseph in long ornate gowns. Wise men in Renaissance clothing bowing down before a very blond-haired, blue-eyed baby. Wooden carvings of the holy family placed amid an African village. And my personal favorite, silhouettes of the people on one side of the manger, with carved woodland creatures—foxes and raccoons and deer—ringing the other.

When the tour is over, Madison tells us we have a few minutes to explore on our own. I go back to the crèche exhibit, sliding into one of the polished side pews and breathing in the quiet. I wonder how many other people have walked these stone floors since the cathedral was built. What would it have been like to be a thirteen-year-old back in the Middle Ages and sit here for prayers? It boggles my mind that the people back then didn't even know America existed. The age of the space falls around me like a heavy blanket. *This* feels like Europe.

"It's pretty intense, isn't it?" Miles is standing next to me, but he's not looking at the nativities. He's staring up at the golden dome that arches overhead. "No matter how many times I come here, I still have to stop and study it. It's supposed to depict the Last Judgment. You know, where everyone is either rewarded or damned for their deeds. I don't know how something so terrifying can be so beautiful."

"I think I know what you mean," I say, letting my gaze rove over all the shimmering colors, undulled by age. "A thousand years. People have been looking up at this for a thousand years!"

"Yeah," Miles says with a half laugh. "It makes you realize how new everything in America is, you know? Europe is really, really old."

"It's kind of nice, though, right? I like old things."

Miles nods. "If you like old things, then you're going to have a great time on this trip." He points back toward the entrance. "Hey, I came to tell you that it's time to meet the others on the front steps."

I wish Madison could be as chill as Miles. I walk quietly back to the cathedral doors with him, wishing I could stay a little bit longer and soak up the silence . . . and age . . . of the place.

Outside in the bright sunlight, Madison and the

others are already waiting.

"Okay!" Madison says from behind her clipboard. "That was fun. Now back to the bus so we aren't late for the next stop!"

The rest of my first day in Florence passes in a blur of fighting off sleep and stumbling back on the bus at different sites. Even Florence's crazy traffic can't keep me awake. Sometimes, I actually get to soak up the sight of the old buildings wreathed in holiday greenery as we drive by, but more often I doze off, waking up when the bus has to brake hard for traffic or when Madison announces that it's time to disembark at another destination, where we inevitably are all forced to endure some icebreaker we've all played a million times already in elementary school. After surviving the attention of other gawking tourists, we're rewarded with another glimpse of Florence's famous history.

I find myself exploring most of these sites solo. The icebreakers must be backfiring, because I don't really feel up for making small talk with the other kids. I want more of what I found in the cathedral. I knew Europe would feel different and foreign and, as Miles said, really, really old. But I didn't expect that feeling to be so magical. We walk through cobblestoned piazzas surrounded by age-smoothed creamy buildings dotted with arches, and cross over the Vasari Corridor with its breathtaking views of the river, and every place we go, I wonder about the countless people who have walked the same streets I'm now walking. What were their lives like? Their families? I imagine all the lives lived here and guess at the little dramas that might have played out for girls in other centuries. Did they go to school? Or stay home to do chores? Or play in the fountains we passed?

My thoughts are interrupted by yet another icebreaker. Too bad it's a total fail. For me, at least. Madison has us match up with someone and then take a few minutes to talk to our partner before introducing them to the entire group. I'm with Kylie, who, of course, has a lot to say, but I don't exactly follow it all. I'm still imagining life in ancient Florence, and by the time she's finished, I realize that I've totally spaced out. So when it's our turn to go, Kylie has tons to share about me—how I like to sketch and paint, how I adore dogs, and how hot chocolate is my favorite drink—but when it's my turn, I realize I can't remember a single thing she's said.

"Um," I say, scrambling to think back to summer camp and what I knew about her then, but my sluggish brain is not working. All the other kids are staring at me. I realize that Kylie is staring at me, too, and she doesn't look annoyed, just a little bit hurt. "Kylie is a great girl," I mumble. "She can text really fast, and she's super excited about things. Really, she's super nice." As I stumble through the introduction, I see Kylie's face go from hurt to embarrassed and a little bit angry. She defensively shoves her phone in her pocket and folds her arms across her chest.

"Sorry," I say when I finally reach the sad conclusion. "I'm super wiped from jet lag. I don't think I'm making very much sense." I smile weakly, but inside I'm cringing. Could I possibly work the word *super* into my vocabulary any more times? Or think of anything lamer to say than "she's a fast texter"? Ugh. I definitely made a mess of that.

It's no surprise that Kylie doesn't try to sit next to me on the bus after that or partner up with me when it's time to wander through the Boboli Garden and see Madison's list of famous statues. In fact, Kylie sticks to Sasha like glue, which, given how everything has gone this afternoon, is completely fine with me.

Finally, at last, when I feel like I can't possibly look at any more statues or endure another icebreaker or handle any more history, the bus pulls up in front of a pearly white building with warm lights shining into the growing dusk. I breathe a huge sigh of relief when Madison's voice announces this destination: the Hotel Savoy.

5

THE HOTEL SAVOY SITS RIGHT on a piazza, so the bus pulls up to the rear entrance, and we all file out. I take in the crisp interior with blurry, sleep-deprived vision. Sleek, modern furniture fills the lobby, and festive garlands of greenery hang from the light fixtures. Madison stops by the front desk and then efficiently passes out our keys with instructions to go to our rooms and rest there until it's time for the cast party. As if I can possibly think of doing anything but sleeping.

When I push open the door to our suite, I see that Mom hasn't been there yet, but all of her luggage is neatly stacked on a chair in the bedroom. My own suitcase is nestled near the opened and made-up sleeper couch in the living area of the suite, and I close the door to the room with a sigh of relief, collapsing on the couch in an exhausted pile.

I wake to a beeping alarm sound and groggily fumble around in my pocket, but I discover that my cell is off. Bleary-eyed, I look around the room, slowly coming to the realization that I'm in Florence and it's late afternoon. It's not an alarm clock that's beeping but the hotel phone, giving out one single tone instead of a normal ring sound. I lift it up with an uncertain "Hello?"

"Christa!"

I rub my eyes with a groan. I already know that no-nonsense voice. *Madison.*

"This is your wake-up call!" Madison says, going on to explain that we need to leave for the cast party dinner in half an hour. "Hope you got a good catnap in! See you soon!"

"Ooomph," I manage before hanging up the phone. It feels like I just fell asleep, but when I check the time, I see that I've crashed for two hours, and it's about seven p.m. Florence time. Which makes it lunchtime back home. After a night of not sleeping. No wonder I feel like I've been run over by a truck.

Stretching, I roll to the edge of the bed. I feel like sand is under my eyelids, and my hair is one staticky tangle. Thirty minutes isn't quite enough time for me to wash my hair and have it dry and presentable, but I'll make the best of it. I stumble to my suitcase and tug on the zipper, which seems stuck on something. With a few tugs, I work it over a bent part with a groan. This suitcase was brand-new! The airline must have damaged it somehow. I flip the lid open and then just stand there, staring. Instead of all the clothes I had packed back at home, I see neat little rolls of fabric, color-coded and lined up from one edge of the case to the other. It's mostly dark colors with some camo and denim thrown in. I stare a little longer until it registers in my sleepy brain. *This isn't my stuff!* I gingerly poke at the clothes, revealing some dark bottles of unfamiliar deodorant and hair product. Definitely a guy suitcase. Somehow there must have been a mix-up at the baggage claim. What am I supposed to do? Change into random guy clothes? Go to the cast party in my airplane-crusty outfit? I shut the lid with a thump.

I reach for the phone to call the lobby. Maybe someone there can contact the airlines. Or, better yet, maybe Madison and Miles have my suitcase floating around somewhere, but before I can dial, there's a knock at the door.

I open the door, expecting to see a maid or Madison or somebody from the hotel staff, but instead Hipster Boy is standing there, looking not airplane-rumpled at all, and even better, he's holding my suitcase! I avoided him as much as possible during the super-awkward icebreakers, so it kind of feels like I'm face-to-face with him for the first time.

He gives me a cute half smile and then introduces himself. "I'm Colby," he says, rolling my suitcase toward the door. "I think this is yours?"

"Ohmigosh, thank you!" I say, and then feel immediately stupid, because I sound like Kylie's clone. "I was just trying to figure out what to do. I found this other bag with all the clothes rolled up in little wads. Wait"—I pause as a horrific thought strikes—"you didn't go through my suitcase, did you?"

"Nah." Colby shrugs. "Didn't need to. I could tell right away it wasn't mine. Yours is newer, I think. And . . ." He grabs the luggage tag. "That's definitely not my handwriting. Way too many loops not to belong to a teenage girl. Plus, the address is American. And I recognized your name, too. The hotel concierge confirmed your suite number, so I said I'd deliver it up to you, and *voilà*." He spreads his arms with a theatrical flourish. "Here we are."

"Cool," I say, wondering if it's cute or creepy that he analyzed my handwriting. Colby runs his hands through his untidy hair. *Definitely cool.*

"So," Colby says while I'm busy looking at him. "Do you have my luggage?"

"Right! Just a sec. Let me get this inside." I turn, and my newly recovered suitcase snags on the doorway. With a few tugs and a ripping sound I force it through, letting it flop on the floor with a thud. But when I go to take Colby his, I can't pull the zipper back up over the bent part. I have to haul it awkwardly to the door, front flapping as I go, and sort of shove it at him. "I think the zipper is broken. I'm sorry. I couldn't get it closed." I feel immediately embarrassed, like he's going to think I've snooped through his underwear or something.

"There's a special trick to it." Colby doesn't seem bothered at all. He stoops and, with a slick maneuver where he leans against one side, zips it up smoothly. "Welp. See you at dinner tonight, then . . . Christa, right?"

"Yup," I say. "It's Christa. Definitely Christa." And then I snap my mouth shut before I say something else. Like I needed the double emphasis. Ugh. Colby leaves, and I spend a few minutes staring at my suitcase and replaying our conversation, thinking of the million more impressive ways I could have introduced myself. Or returned his luggage to him. But then I realize that my prep time is down from half an hour to only twenty minutes, and I've got to get ready.

Passing the full-length mirror on the way to the bathroom, I shriek. I seriously have just had my first conversation with a kid on this trip—apart from Kylie, who totally doesn't count—while looking like a walking disaster. I've got a big spot where I spilled Coke on my collar, and then my mascara has smeared under one eye, which gives me the freakish look of a winking raccoon. Add to that the fact that my hair mashed up on one side while I slept. No wonder he was looking at me funny.

"Ohmigosh," I channel Kylie and say to my reflection. "You are such a weirdo."

6

I WEAR MY CUTE BLACK dress and my tamest ugly Christmas sweater—the cardigan with little ornaments all over it—to the actors' cast party. Mom was right: Acqua al 2, tonight's restaurant, *is* fancy. The theater troupe has reserved a special room in the wine cellar, and I stand on the edges, taking in the scene. The weathered brick walls are covered with hand-painted plates filled with landscapes and things written in Italian. The curved stone ceilings flicker with the lit candles that are arranged between place settings. Ivy-dotted red berries decorate our long table in the center. The grown-ups seem more comfortable in this environment—some already are sitting down munching appetizers, while others stand mingling, glasses in hand while they laugh about the funny things that can go wrong with international travel and ooh and aah over the differ-ent bottles of wine on display. I can tell that, like me, most of the other kids don't know exactly what to do. Kylie has cornered Sasha at the far end of the room, but I'm not sure if I really want to just walk up and insert myself into their conversation. Besides, I might need to wake up a bit more before I can handle the Kylie-gushing.

Instead, I decide to try to find my spot at the table. Madison has marked off one side of it for the kids with hand-lettered place cards above the round plates. My place is at the very end on the other side of Harry Potter Kid and Spiky Hair.

"Hey, guys," I say as I slide into my seat.

"Hi," Spiky Hair says as he points at himself. "I'm Logan."

"Hi, Logan," I say. "I'm Christa."

Harry Potter Kid introduces himself as Owen. Both boys clean up well. Owen looks like he's adopted some mixture of British and H&M style with his striped car-digan and corduroys. Logan is chill, wearing jeans and a button-up shirt with a skinny tie.

Owen swivels to face me. "We were just talking about our favorite Harry Potter book. Mine is *Order of the Phoe-nix*, but I know that's pretty rare." He sounds pleased with himself. "Some people hate it, you know. Harry gets so angsty."

I share a smile with Logan, who fake whispers, "*Save me!*" but Owen only rolls his eyes.

"So? What's your favorite?"

"We-ell," I say, drawing it out. "Don't kill me, but I haven't actually read the books."

Owen's mouth drops open, and I hold up my hands defensively. "I'm more of a movie girl, okay? I've seen them all. Lots of times. The last one is awesome, but the third one is totally my favorite. That scene where Hermione punches Malfoy? Perfectly executed."

While Owen sits silent, brow furrowed as if he's trying to compute the fact that someone hasn't actually read the books, Logan and I start chatting. "I can't tell if it's morning or night. I'm so mixed up from the jet lag."

"I know! That was my first all-nighter!" he says with a grin. "I'm glad you joined us. There's only so much Harry Potter talk I can take!"

"Hey!" Owen says as he tosses a crusty wedge from the bread basket at Logan. "You told me you were a fan."

"I am." Logan reaches for the little plate that has a circle of olive oil pooled on it. "Just not a superfan."

"I'm starved," I say. Now that I can smell the fresh bread,

I realize that whatever time it is back home, my stomach is chiming *ravenous*. And thank goodness they have some normal bread. I bypass the sketchy-looking pasta dish that makes up the first course and dump most of the bread basket onto my plate. Too bad there's not any butter, but olive oil is totally on my safe list. I can live off bread if I have to. Which, when I see the server coming up with the entrée, I realize might very well be the case. He's carrying plates of the restaurant's signature dish: blueberry steak.

I stare at my serving. Blueberries I can handle. I kind of even like steak. But the two mixed together? Um, is the chef having an off day? I don't want to be rude, especially since this is an über-fancy restaurant, but the thing on my plate looks like a cross between a chocolate lava cake and a brick drowned in mud. Seriously. Even the pretty little garnish of cucumber and a radish rose, valiantly trying to rescue it from disaster, just look sad.

I glance over at the boys, but they are wolfing it down, so I'm guessing they don't care.

"This is so good," Logan says around a mouthful of food.

"It's brilliant." Owen shovels in another bite. "It's the kind of thing they might serve at Hogwarts."

I say nothing and reach for the heel of the loaf of bread.

"Not a fan of fruity steak?" a voice says at my elbow. I look over to see Colby sliding into the seat next to me, wearing a T-shirt with a tuxedo front printed on it and camouflage pants. "It's not as bad as it looks." He swaps the place card next to me, which reads "Madison," with his own. I hope Madison won't care—she and Miles are over with the grown-ups.

"I'll take your word for it." I push my plate back an inch. "Do you want mine?"

He holds up his hands with a laugh. "Better than it sounds doesn't mean that it's my favorite."

"So you've been here before?"

"Four times, to be exact. My dad is always traveling," he explains, pointing at a small, nicely dressed man who is sitting at the other end of the table. It's Nic, the director. "He usually tours through Europe at least once a year, which means I do, too."

"That's cool," I begin, but Kylie has somehow appeared at Colby's other side and cuts me off.

"Ohmigosh," she says, looking up at him with a smile plastered on her face. Kylie is decked out with full-on makeup, perfect hair, and a shimmery sleeveless shirt and leather circle skirt. "You are *so* lucky. I've been to New York with my dad on tour, but that's nothing like Europe.

And every year! Sasha, did you hear that?" She reaches behind her to tug on Sasha's sleeve, directing her to sit down next to her.

I can't tell if Sasha is cool with Kylie's BFF-ness or if she's secretly looking for escape, but she doesn't say much. She's wearing an all-black dress with a high neck and cute lace-up boots.

I nod at her. "I like your boots."

"Thanks," she says, and it looks as if she might continue, but Kylie is already talking, launching into a rave over how delicious the blueberry steak tastes.

"I'm such a foodie, you know." Kylie giggles. "I absolutely adore the Cooking Channel. My friends are all: Kylie, that's BORING. And I'm all, *food is never boring!*"

I reach for my water, embarrassed for Kylie. She's just trying way too hard.

"My dad says eating in Europe can be an adventure," I say, trying to rescue Kylie from herself.

"Oh, that's so true. Jamie Oliver—he's my favorite chef, he's *so* great, isn't he?—says that, too." She stops gushing for a minute, as if she's just noticed that I'm not eating the blueberry steak. "Is something wrong with yours, Christa?"

I reach for another roll. "Nothing some more of this

bread can't fix. I don't know if it's an adventure to eat it, but Florence might possibly have the best bread in the world."

"Just wait until you get to Paris." Colby beckons to a server to bring more.

"You've been to Paris? Lucky!" Kylie says, and I'm not sure I can take much more of the conversation. Logan and Owen have moved on from Harry Potter to soccer teams, and Sasha is studying the room as if she's making mental notes on how to write a report on everything later.

"Excuse me," I say, getting up to find the bathroom. I grab my cell and snap a picture of the untouched blueberry steak on my plate to text to Dad. I wonder if he'll still think Europe has such great food options when he sees the combination of berries and beef. Ugh. I also take a pic of the walls crowded with individual plates. I walk down one hallway, but the sounds coming from behind the only door are kitchen noises, so I try a side passageway.

I duck around a corner and glance up from my cell to see the worst sight possible for any thirteen-year-old girl to see. My mom. And Todd. Making out. I stand there, frozen in place, and it feels like I'm in some sort of nightmare. Mom is kissing someone else. I mean, really, really kissing him, like I haven't seen her kiss Dad in . . . well, ever. I feel a hot flare of anger in my stomach. How long has this been going on—this her-and-Todd thing? I step backward, and my fingers fumble with my phone. Mom and Todd are so "occupied" that they don't notice I'm there, and because it's so quiet in this corner, I can even hear the kissing sounds. Which only makes me madder. I back out of there fast, passing the kitchen doors and speeding down the hallway, brushing by a server who smiles and points me toward the bathroom on the other end.

I stumble through the door and lean up against the cool tiled walls. I can't stop replaying what I just saw.

SOS, I text my best friend, Dani. It's afternoon in Chicago, which means Dani is still in school and shouldn't check her cell phone, but I know she'd absolutely risk detention over this. **Major parent crisis moment. Saw Mom kissing guy from the cast. And not acting. Help!!!**

But Dani must be actually following school rules, because no text comes back, despite our promise always to respond immediately to any SOS. I shove my phone away and wash my hands so I have something to do in case someone randomly walks into the bathroom. In the mirror, I see that I look the same as I did earlier despite the fact that everything has just hopped a train to Crazy-town. Are Mom and Todd dating? Is *he* why she wanted a divorce in the first place? Is *he* the "different thing" she had been wanting?

I try to smooth out my hair. I feel the tears coming,

like I might just start flat-out sobbing in the bathroom, and I try to rein myself in. I mean, come *on*, Christa. You know that your parents aren't getting back together. That is not new information anymore. But I cry anyway, holding the sobs back so tears just leak out the corners of my eyes. Okay, so maybe some tiny part of me has always hoped they might work it out and get back together, because why not? Sometimes it happens. Okay, it never happens. But this? This is final. And seeing Todd and Mom together is like taking a big fat neon highlighter to the fact that my parents' marriage is totally over and that this is my new normal. Me split in two with half of me back in Chicago and half of me in some fancy bathroom in Europe knowing, like really, really knowing, that it's over. Mom has moved on. Like seriously moved on. So much so that she's getting very merry with this Todd person.

My tears turn into a sort of half cry, half laugh as I think about how ridiculous it is that I walked in on them, like a parent catching teenagers making out. I grab a paper towel and wipe my eyes, replaying the scene in my mind, and a giggle escapes. I'm the one who should be sneaking off for her first kiss! Ohmigosh! What if Mom had looked up and seen me?

I re-create what my face might have been like, trying

out different shocked and disgusted variations in the mirror, and the tight feeling at the back of my throat lessens. My eyes are a little red, but at least I'm not crying anymore. Then, right when I'm in the middle of the best nose-wrinkled, very appalled face, Sasha comes in.

"Are you okay, Christa?" Sasha asks in a quiet, concerned sort of way.

I laugh and wonder if it's worth attempting to explain. "Totally. Just trying to get over a very weird moment with my mom." I turn around and lean up against the edge of the countertop. Sasha isn't Dani. In fact, I barely even know her, but maybe it would help to purge all the whatever-it-is-I'm-feeling. I open my mouth to start explaining when the door swings open a second time and Kylie bounces in.

"Girl party in the bathroom!" she says, pumping her hands in the air in an exaggerated dance move. "Why didn't you guys invite me?"

Sasha rolls her eyes. "There's no party. Some of us just need to use the bathroom." And she pushes back toward the stalls.

"Right. So isn't this cast party fab?" Kylie continues, bustling over to the mirror and whipping out some extra-volume mascara. "I mean, the food is amazing, and the atmosphere is so . . ." She stumbles over her superlatives.

"Well, so . . . amazingly European. And the guys." She puts the mascara wand back in with a flourish and turns to face me. "Aren't the guys so cute? Did you see that Colby kid is wearing camo? I *love* guys who wear camo."

"I hadn't noticed," I say. I wish I could tell Kylie to just chill. That she doesn't need to try so hard. And that there's more to this trip than the boys.

"They're about to serve dessert." Kylie rummages in her makeup bag for lipstick. "You won't want to miss out. Besides"—she gives me a sideways look—"Logan seems to think you're pretty cool."

I snort. "Logan just doesn't want to be left alone in Harry Potter land."

"I know, right?" Kylie says, fiddling with her hair. "I mean, who doesn't like Harry Potter, but that Owen kid is mega obsessed."

"They're pretty *nice* boys," I say, hoping that Kylie will catch my drift. I grab the door and open it for her. I'm not sure I can take any more boy-crazy conversations with Kylie, but that may be better than the alternative of actually talking to Mom. As I reenter the dining room, I have to pass by her. She's chatting with Colby's dad, Nic, as though everything is normal. Todd is standing next to her, but he's not even listening. He's scrolling through his cell log. Like they weren't just sucking face a few minutes ago. Okay, so maybe it wasn't that intense, but still, a kiss is a kiss. And somehow that makes me even angrier. Did she break up our family for nothing? He'd better mean something to her! But then I change my mind. I'm not ready for anyone but Dad to mean something to Mom! And now I'm obsessing over all of the places it could go. Here we are about to tour through the most romantic countries in the world, and Mom and Todd are together. I stop in my tracks as I see Kylie smile at her dad as she passes him. *Kylie.* Todd's daughter. If Mom and Todd get together, that means Kylie and I . . . no, I can't even go there.

Mom sees me then. "Having a good time, sweetie?" she says over her shoulder.

Not as good as you, I think. But I say "Sure," because if I actually talk to her she'll see the fact that I *saw* her and Todd written all over my face. And the only thing worse than seeing your mom kissing her new man is having to talk to her about it.

I stalk back to the table and plop down in my chair. There's some kind of weird fruit tart and a big scoop of gelato waiting for me. The other kids are still in their places, and Colby fills me in that everyone is saying what they're most looking forward to seeing in Florence. I smell my gelato, which, as if the universe is sending me a peace offering, is happily and familiarly chocolate. I try to listen to the conversation. Logan is talking about some famous bridge, and Owen hopes we'll be able to go on a gondola ride, but every time I try to engage, my gaze is drawn back to the other side of the room to watch Mom and Todd.

Todd is totally leaning in too close. And there's no way that arm draped behind her chair is a normal friendly one. He is so trying to impress Mom. He smiles at her, the kind of smile that doesn't even show his teeth, a smug smile that makes me want to throw my fruit tart at him. It's like he's already *with* Mom, like she belongs with him. How long have they been in the same theater group? At *least* two years, since I've been to camp with Kylie for that long. I scowl at Todd. Maybe he's been into Mom for a long time.

"What's the matter?" Colby asks in a low voice while Owen and Logan start arguing over whether Florence even has gondolas.

"Nothing," I say, but my fuming thoughts at Todd finally bubble over and come out of my mouth. "Just that too-perfect Todd is hitting on my mom." I scrunch up my nose. "He *is* too perfect, isn't he? Who has hair that stays back in a wave like that? And that grin? I bet he uses tooth-whitening toothpaste. Ugh. I can't believe that my mom is falling for someone so vain." Todd is leaning toward Mom again, smiling that smug smile at her as if they are a couple.

"Wait, what? Todd? You mean that guy over there?" Colby sounds confused.

I take a minute to fill him in on what I just saw. It feels good to purge.

"Okay, okay. Put the spoon down." Colby lays his hand on mine, and for the first time I realize I've been hostilely stirring my gelato as if it's an enemy. Now it's just a puddle of mush oozing over to the soggy but untouched tart on my plate.

"Oops," I say weakly, glancing around to see if anyone else has noticed my weirdness, but they are all engaged in the Great Gondola Argument.

"Come with me," Colby says. "I think I know something that might help."

7

COLBY LEADS ME PAST THE alcove where I saw Mom and Todd—ew, unwelcome visual reminder, thankyouverymuch—and up the stairs to a big window that looks out over the Florence street. We're high enough that I can see a little ways off, and the twinkling lights of the old city look enchanting.

"Isn't it great?" Colby says, pointing out the Boboli Garden, which he says is one of his favorite places. "No matter how many times I've come to Florence, there's always more to explore." He turns to me with a half smile. "See? What's going on with your mom and Todd is—well—your mom and Todd. Don't let it ruin your trip, you know?"

Is he for real? What he says sounds super grown-up, but that doesn't make it untrue. I press a palm up against the cold window, as if I could take all that old magic into myself.

"You're right. Cheesy line or not"—Colby raises an eyebrow at this, but I continue—"it's up to me whether I let whatever it is that's going on with too-perfect, smug Todd and Mom bother me." I get a brilliant idea. "In fact, from here on out, He Who Must Not Be Named shall henceforth be referred to as S.T.," I say in my most theatrical voice. "You know, for 'Smug Todd.'"

Colby grins. "Like a code name, right?"

"Exactly! *You'll* know who I'm talking about, and *I'll* know who I'm talking about, but no one else will. And if I start talking about it too much, well, you can remind me not to obsess, okay? Now. No more S.T. Tell me why you love the Boboli Garden so much. And, for the love of everything good, *are* there gondolas in Florence?"

Colby laughs out loud. He has a nice laugh, and just hearing it makes me feel less anxious about S.T. and Mom.

"Well," he says. "The Boboli Garden has the best gelato cart in all the city, with flavors I bet you've never tried, like lavender and basil lemon and salted caramel."

"Ooh, I like salted caramel," I say. "Chicago's got some pretty fancy food, too, you know." I don't tell him that there's no possible way I'm going to eat lavender anything.

"But plain old vanilla is really my favorite."

After a little while, Colby and I return to the other kids, who have moved on from the Great Gondola Argument and are now talking about their most embarrassing moments. (In case you're wondering, Colby told me that it's Venice that's famous for gondolas, although Florence has a few touristy ones.)

Kylie is midstory about somehow walking around in front of a cute guy with her underwear on her foot. A mean part of me wonders if she did it on purpose to get his attention, but I don't say so. Out of the corner of my eye, I see Todd and my mom sharing their dessert, and I lose track of Kylie's story. My mom *never* eats dessert.

"S.T. makes another move," I whisper to Colby, who leans in close to hear.

"But does S.T. have underwear on his shoe?" Colby says back in a low voice, and I almost snort ice water out my nose. This leads to a fit of coughing after which even Kylie stops talking long enough to ask me if I'm okay, I pull it together.

"Don't," I croak at Colby when it looks like he's going to say something else. I can tell by his now-familiar half smile that a joke is coming. Instead, he turns to the waiter who is coming around and asking if we'd like anything else.

"Do you have any vanilla gelato?" he asks.

How sweet is he? The rest of the night isn't too bad. The gelato is incredibly good, and Colby is fun to hang out with, and the rest of the kids are getting along really well. Eventually Madison comes over to round us up.

"Time to go back to the hotel," she says. It turns out the grown-ups are staying a little longer at the restaurant, so we all say a collective good night before boarding our minibus, which will take us back to the hotel. When I pass him, S.T. offers me a friendly smile, but I pretend I don't see and stare past his shoulder at the plates on the wall. No way am I going to be nice to the guy who probably split up my mom and dad. Fortunately, I don't have to do more than wave at my mom.

Back in the suite, it's time for my first Skype call with Dad. Good thing the suite's bathroom is also four-star and humongo, because I'd rather call him from there and have some privacy in case Mom comes back. It's late in Florence but only midafternoon in Chicago. Dad is at his office desk sipping coffee from his old brown mug and smiling at me.

"How's it going, Pumpkin?" he says. "Italy still as beautiful as ever?"

As soon as I see his face, I realize how far away Chicago really is. Like across an ocean on another continent far away. But I launch into a recounting of the day's events— with detailed descriptions of the octagonal roof and the horrible icebreakers all the way through to the cast party and Colby showing me the Florence skyline, omitting, of course, The Kiss.

"That sounds about right for a whirlwind day in Florence," Dad says with a grin. "I think you're in good hands with Madison. She came highly recommended from Student Tours International. I suggested to Nic that she'd be a great fit for this trip."

"*You* are responsible for Madison?" I frown. "Dad. She's got a clipboard. And color-coded itineraries. And *icebreakers.*"

He laughs. "And what's wrong with a clipboard?"

"Whatever." It feels nice to banter with Dad. Like a little bit of parental normalness after Mom's total betrayal at the restaurant.

"Besides, I know someone who color-codes their Christmas plans."

I know Dad is just teasing, but it still stings that he seems to have forgotten that the Best Christmas Plan Ever is forever tied up with the horrible night when they told me about the divorce. I give him a weak laugh. "Yeah, but that's for *Christmas.*"

"So," he says. "Tell me about the other kids. This Colby sounds cool."

I suddenly feel defensive. *Have I been talking about Colby too much?* Dad's voice sounds suspiciously curious, like he's implying a million little things without saying anything.

"He's nice. He's just a boy on the trip." I make sure to tell him about Owen, Logan, and Sasha as well. "And you remember Kylie, right?"

He must be able to tell by my tone that I'm not a huge fan. "I thought you liked her. Weren't you at summer camp or something together? Kylie—what's her last name . . . Barrows, right? Todd's daughter! Nice people."

"Yeah." I wonder if he would still think so if he knew Todd was kissing Mom. "Well, it's hard to figure out the real Kylie. She's nice enough; she's just so intense and talks like a mile a minute, and it seems like everything she's doing is to get attention, you know?"

"Mmm," Dad says. "Maybe she could use a friend."

Which is such a parent thing to say. How am I supposed to be Kylie's friend when she's so shallow and I can't even have a real conversation with her? And, if I'm honest, when I don't really want to be her friend?

Dad's looking at his watch and saying he has a meeting soon. "I'm glad you're having fun, Chris. And look!" He holds up a travel brochure. Printed across the front in flowy script it says: *Vasile Tours: Allow the unexpected to lead you somewhere you were always meant to go.*

"Dad. You did not. That is so corny."

"And true." He raises his coffee mug to toast me before signing off. "Love you, Chris."

"Love you, too, Dad," I say, and then we end the call.

I can't believe he's marketing that cheesy slogan. I pull out my cell to text Dani as much when I see that I somehow missed her response to my SOS text from earlier.

Your mom and the hot guy? she's written. **Go, Jocelyn!** followed by little smiley emojis with heart eyes.

Ugh. Dani can be so clueless sometimes. I decide not to text her back tonight after all. It sounds like a lot of work to explain to her that S.T., while theoretically hot for an old guy, is not a win for Jocelyn. Or for our family. Which immediately makes me feel guilty. Shouldn't I want my mom to be happy?

I wash my face and then climb between the cool sheets that have been neatly turned down by the hotel staff. Someone has even left a little piece of chocolate on my pillow, and, after examining it to make sure there are no hidden nuts, I almost eat it. But, really, there's no wrapper, so how am I supposed to know what's inside? I toss it at the hotel trash can and lie back down. You'd think that because I'm so exhausted, I'd be able to fall asleep right away. But nope.

Apparently that's not how jet lag works. Instead, I lie in bed trying not to think about S.T. and Mom for a long time. When that doesn't work, I replay all the things I saw today, landing on the incredible view of the city Colby showed me at the restaurant, until I finally fall asleep.

8

I'M MID-DREAM IN A SCENE where a crazy-looking Kylie is chasing me with a blueberry steak screaming, "Try it! It's epicurean!" while S.T. and Madison point and laugh at me when someone knocks at the restaurant door. Which is when—*duh*—I realize that it's a dream, and one I'm super glad is over. I wrap the throw blanket around my shoulders and peer through the peephole to see one of the hotel employees standing outside looking way too awake for the middle of the night.

"Signorina Vasile?" he says in an authoritative voice. "It's Tom. From the front desk. I have a delivery for you."

I open the door a smidgen.

"*Buongiorno*," he says, which is when I realize that it's not actually the middle of the night, I'm just jet-lagged.

And then I perk up because he's holding one of my favorite things ever . . . a *Christmas present!*

I thank him and take my present inside, where I flip on a dim light and plop down on my bed to examine it. The package is wrapped in white lace-patterned paper and tied with a red ribbon. Mysteriously, there's no name on the tag to indicate who it's from.

There's an important ritual to opening any package. First, you slip your fingers through the folded triangles on the ends and loosen the tape. Then you work on the middle. I savor the moment, carefully removing the pretty wrapping to reveal a white box. I lift the lid and fold back the red tissue paper inside. Immediately, the tinny sound of a mechanized song emerges, and something wiggles. I slam the lid down with a muffled squeal and glance over to Mom's room to see if it woke her, but it's still all silent and dark in there.

What is in the box? I take the whole thing into the bathroom and slowly lift the lid. The tacky music continues, morphing into an awful version of "Jingle Bell Rock," but I almost don't hear it because I'm stupefied by the even tackier dancing Santa jiggling inside. Santa is wearing jeans and a red-and-green flannel shirt, with silvery suspenders on his wiggling belly. *What the heck?* There's a little Santa gift tag tied around his wrist. It's not signed, but I'd recognize the handwriting anywhere. *Dad!* Printed in his characteristic block letters is a message: WELCOME TO THIS YEAR'S GREAT VASILE SCAVENGER HUNT: THE TWELVE DARES OF CHRISTA. #1: DARE YOU TO DANCE AT THE PIAZZA SANTA CROCE.

Eeeeee! We *are* going to do a scavenger hunt this year! I can't believe that Dad figured out a way to pull this off. I drop the Santa, looking around the bathroom stupidly, as though he might pop out from behind the fancy shower. *Wait. Is Dad here?* I know it's crazy, but he's the king of crazy surprises. I leap up, leaving Santa's dancing bootie half in, half out of the box, and dash for my cell phone.

Where are you? I text. A few minutes pass before I get his misspelled response.

Chris? Anything okay?

And then my foggy brain wakes up enough to realize that it's impossible for him to be here. I saw him Skype from his office a few hours ago, and even Dad couldn't pull off a transatlantic flight in a few hours. Besides, from his incoherent reply, I can tell I've woken him up.

Your package came, I write. **That Santa is SO bad. I'm just saying.**

Ha! he writes back. **I knew you'd love him. Continue**

him your first friend on this year's diving salamander hunt.

What?

A few seconds later he clarifies. **Stupid autocorrect. Consider him your first find on this year's daring SCAVEN-GER HUNT.**

I'm in, I text back, and as I do, I realize that I so totally am. I mean, despite everything, I've been trying my best to be all excited about this trip, but I haven't realized how truly sad I was to be missing everything back at home until this very moment. Being able to still do the scavenger hunt in Europe is like having a little piece of home-Christmas here with me. **Thanks, Dad. Sorry to wake you up. Go back to bed.**

Have fun, Chris!

I rescue Santa from his box and flip off his motion-activated switch so he stops jiggling. I read the tag again. Now to figure out what the Piazza Santa Croce is. It sounds familiar, and my sluggish brain thinks I recognize the name from yesterday's whirlwind city tour, but I'll need Mom's guidebooks to be sure. With Santa securely off dancing mode, I creep into her side of the suite. Daylight peeks from behind the heavy draperies just enough for me to pick my way over to the side where her bags are.

Mom is completely zonked, wearing her black travel

eye-cover thingies that make me think of old-fashioned movie stars. With all the excitement of the scavenger hunt news, I had almost forgotten about last night, but when I see her, everything comes flooding back in, and all I can think of is The Kiss. I wonder how late she stayed up. I wonder if she spent all the rest of her time at the restaurant. With S.T.

I spot her cell phone perched on her nightstand. Does she have S.T.'s number stored in there? *Of course she does.* They're castmates. But what other dirt might I find?

I feel a twinge of guilty conscience. I know it isn't right to spy on her phone, but I reach for it anyway. Mom's obviously not interested in telling me about S.T. How else am I supposed to find out the truth?

But just as I try to pick it up, Mom's alarm buzzes, sounding crazy-loud in the room, and sends me jumping two feet backward.

Mom groans, groping blindly for the nightstand to smack the snooze button. My guess is that I have three snoozes before she actually wakes up. Guiltily, I grab the guidebook from her carry-on bag and retreat to my side of the suite, shoving it, Santa, the dare, and the other things I want for the day into my backpack. By the time the third snooze sounds I've showered and dressed in my cute jeans paired with my favorite reindeer sweater and red-and-green scarf. Because: Christmas!

"I'm going down to breakfast," I tell Mom when she finally stumbles from her room, hair pushed back crazily with her eye covers as she beelines it for the mini coffee-maker in the bathroom.

"Okay," she says groggily. Mom is always super out of it until she gets caffeine in her. "Don't leave the hotel, okay?"

"I won't." I grab the itinerary I got yesterday. "But the kid group tour starts in thirty minutes. I'm supposed to go with them, right?"

"Um." Mom grunts in my direction. "Yeah. Go with them. Rehearsal for me. Opening night tonight. Stay with Madison."

Mom keeps talking in little bursts like that, but I get what she means. Besides, Madison has already clearly outlined everything. When the grown-ups are in rehearsal or performance, we're either sleeping, having "free time" at the hotel, or with the kid tour. I try to believe what Dad said last night, that Madison is a good tour guide, and we're going to have fun.

In the hotel breakfast room, things are pretty quiet. Some of the other actors are already there, with none of the joviality from the night before. Instead, everyone looks tired. Which isn't too surprising. In all the years Mom's been acting, I've yet to meet a morning person in the theater.

The buffet is filled with wedges of strange cheeses and thinly sliced meat that looks like salami. Obviously, I skip those and grab an apple from the fruit bowl instead. They also have what looks like plain cornflakes—no thanks— and some boiled eggs. Double no. Good thing I've brought plenty of my favorite granola bars from back home. I usually eat two of those for breakfast anyway.

I find a little table near a window and settle in, pulling out the guidebook and my food. A waiter appears at my side with a tiny cup and saucer, which he proceeds to fill with thick brown coffee. I'm not a big coffee drinker, but it's okay enough as long as there aren't any surprise ingredients in it. Besides, Dad is a coffee addict, and I think of him as I dump in three huge scoops of sugar.

The guidebook tells me that the Piazza Santa Croce is a beautiful square in the heart of the city, where street musicians play traditional Italian music. It gets its name from the basilica, which as best I can tell is a fancy church that has sixteen chapels and a statue of Dante out front. There's nothing about dancing. Or Santas. I gulp down more coffee. What is Dad actually daring me to do? I have a sneaking suspicion that whatever dancing in the piazza will be, it might have something to do with the little pep talk he gave me before we left.

Dad seems serious about this "allow the unexpected to lead you someplace you were always meant to go" deal. The unexpected and I aren't exactly on friendly terms right now, so I feel a little antsy inside, somewhere between excitement and anxiety, but let's be honest, the anxiety has totally been winning lately. I wonder what Dad would say if I told him I won't do the dares. But at the thought of that I feel like crying. No matter what, I can't bail on the one thing that will keep me connected to home this Christmas, however scary. I take a deep breath, reach for my cell phone, and send Dad a quick text: **Dare #1 accepted.**

9

ONCE I'M ON THE BUS with the other kids I feel like my text might have been premature. What was I thinking? There's no way I want to do something unexpected! And how exactly am I supposed to even get to the piazza in the first place? Colby takes the seat next to me, oblivious to my internal wishy-washy-ness, and he picks up where we left off the night before, pointing out some of his favorite spots in the city while we halfway listen to Madison's good-morning talk.

"We are going to have so much fun today!" she says brightly.

"They shouldn't turn the microphones on until later in the morning," I mumble.

"I've been on two trips with M&M. They're not so bad," Colby confides.

"M&M?"

"Madison and Miles. Well, I've been on lots more with Miles, but not since he became in charge and everything. His dad and my dad have been working together forever. So he used to be sitting in our seats. Madison, not so much. You think she's intense now, you should have seen her on her first trip. Believe me, she's mellowing."

I find that hard to imagine. Especially when the bus pulls up to Galleria dell'Accademia, and Madison launches into lecture mode about how American tourists are always obnoxious in European cities.

"We are *not* going to be that kind of group," she bosses. "Be polite. Follow instructions. Stick together."

It all seems simple enough until we unload and see that the Galleria is *packed* with other tourists: groups of elderly people, unhappy-looking families, smooching couples. Not the reminder I needed. Inside, it's not much better. Our group merges with the others and begins inching through the exhibit rooms. Wood floors and light-colored walls combine with high ceilings that arch over the exhibits. Clusters of people slowly shuffle from each painting and sculpture and make everything feel crowded and slow-moving. Huge oil paintings in ornate gilded frames line the walls, and in the center of each room beautiful white stone sculptures tower above the tourists.

In one room an artist has set up a portable easel and is trying to re-create the masterpiece in front of her. Back home, I used to camp out in the modern art wing of the Art Institute of Chicago and try different techniques, and watching the woman paint sends a pang of homesickness through me—both for Chicago and for the art I haven't created in weeks. I hurry past her into another room that is all oils, some of which are over three hundred years old. I wonder if the artists could have ever imagined that people centuries later would be studying their work. I stop in front of an image of a storm-tossed sea that's all gray and black with a harsh line of the setting sun gashed across the horizon. I read the descriptions next to the painting, struck by the way the artist used shading to emphasize the fury of the waves and the calm of the open sea beyond. I mean, sometimes a painting just looks like a painting. But other times it's so much more than that, and I stay by that piece until I feel some of the ancient calm of the open sea.

And don't even get me started on the sculptures—the way the light hits the curves of musculature, the hours and hours of painstaking work for each one, the incredible skill it took to make stone look so alive. There are several pieces by the famed Michelangelo, and I am glad to see that all the kids are able to be somewhat mature about the fact that many of them aren't, well, wearing clothes. Okay, so there's minimal giggling coming from Kylie's direction, but it's Kylie.

After the third room, I'm overwhelmed, like when you eat a really rich dessert and are super stuffed and someone brings out a whole tray of more sweets. I have no room for more art. I've reached art-appreciation capacity. All the paintings are starting to look alike, and my legs are getting tired. I wish there were more benches to sit down on. Logan and Owen must be thinking along the same lines, because they are laughing and joking with Kylie and Sasha one minute and the next they are down on all fours, flattening their backs into one long bench and motioning for the girls to sit down. I'm stuck behind a clog of German tourists who are taking a really, really long time with the next exhibit, and they block my view before I can see what happens next.

Then the German tourists move, and I automatically step forward, my face pointed ahead but my gaze riveted on the unfolding scene with the other kids. Madison has discovered them. From where I'm standing I can hear bits of her lecture. "What I was talking about . . . loud Americans . . . no respect . . . appreciation for art and other cultures." The other kids are listening to her, but they keep shooting suppressed smiles at each other.

Just then, Colby says something from by my shoulder, and I snap my attention forward, realizing that I've been standing at the statue forever. I've been watching the other kids, but to everyone else it looks like I've been gaping at a statue of a completely naked man, Michelangelo's famous *David*. And it's not like my face is pointed at his face either.

"Ohmigosh," I say, realization dawning as I stumble to the side, bumping up against the plexiglass wall around the statue. It looks like I'm a total perv. And it's so much worse that Colby is right there trying to be all normal.

"Christa?" he asks. "Everything okay?"

Um, besides feeling totally stupid? I'm trying to think of a witty reply when I hear a really, really, *really* unwelcome sound. From somewhere very close by the tinny refrain of "Jingle Bell Rock" is recognizable. And then my backpack starts squirming.

"Ohmigosh! Ohmigosh! Ohmigosh!" is all I can say as I fumble with the pack's zippers. I must have somehow bumped the stupid Santa's motion switch. "Oh no!" I barely get a grasp on the zipper before it sticks even more. Now the bag is open a tiny bit, making the music louder, but I can't fit my hand in to get at the switch to turn the thing off. "What do I do?" I hiss at Colby, who is staring at me with a suspicious half smile.

"Seriously!" I can see security guards moving from their sleepy posts in the doorway to investigate the sound. "Help!"

The buzz of the crowd grows quiet as people around me check cell phones to make sure they're not responsible. I can hear Madison's voice more clearly now, still talking to the other kids.

"Ohmigosh, Madison! Her head is going to explode when she finds out!" A tacky dancing Santa that I can't shut off is way worse than Logan and Owen's display from earlier.

"This way," Colby says, tugging on my elbow and cutting across the crowded room to an empty hallway near the restrooms. I slump down to the floor, yanking the backpack open, breaking the zipper in the process, and finally switch off the doll. I feel like throwing jolly old St. Nick into the trash.

"Why do you have that thing?"

I'm not looking at Colby, but I can hear laughter in his voice. And now that the initial panic and wave of embarrassment is over, I can see the funny part, too. I start to giggle.

"Did you see the look on Madison's face?"

Colby bulges out his eyes in a fair imitation and starts miming the way she was hunting for the source of the sound, and I laugh even harder. Now that the awful music is silenced, the buzz of tourist conversation returns, along with my normal heart rate. I shove sleeping Santa back in my bag and tell Colby why I have him.

"It's kind of a tradition with Dad and me. Every Christmas at home Dad plans a scavenger hunt for me and my friends. There are usually twelve things, you know, like 'on the first day of Christmas . . .'"

"Gotcha," Colby says. "That sounds cool."

It *is* cool. It's one of my many favorite things about Christmastime, and, as I tell Colby about past scavenger hunts, I realize again how glad I am that the scavenger hunt is one thing that's going to stay the same this Christmas. "Even though I'm all the way here in Europe, this year's scavenger hunt has twelve dares for me to complete." Out of nowhere, I feel like I might cry. *What the heck?* I look down at Santa and blink back the tears. Santa's painted-on smile seems to be gloating at all the trouble he's caused. "This Santa is *so* ridiculous, isn't he?" I give a watery laugh.

"No doubt," Colby says, fake punching Santa's cherry-red nose. "Your dad is pretty crazy to dare you to set him off in the middle of a museum."

"Ha! That wasn't exactly the dare. More of a technical

difficulty." I explain about Piazza Santa Croce. "But I don't know how I'm supposed to get to the piazza, or what it means to dance there."

"I do," Colby says, almost too casually. "If you want some help, that is."

"Okay," I say slowly. It would be nice to not be doing the dares alone. "If you're sure you don't mind."

"Nah, it'll be fun. I know where the piazza is and everything."

"Really?" I glance up at his face. He looks totally pleased. "How do you know all of that stuff anyway?"

He runs his hands through his hair a little bit sheepishly. "So I know we kind of laugh at what an intense tour director Madison is. But, um, I kind of want to be one when I grow up. I mean, not, well, not like Madison, obviously."

I stare at him. He's kind of cute when he's all flustered. "You want to be a tour guide?"

He nods. "I love traveling. I love exploring new places and telling other people how to have the perfect adventures."

"Okay, now you're starting to sound like my dad." I tell him how Dad owns his own travel agency.

"Your dad sounds cool. But really, I know all about the city and can help you find hotels, ticket offices—whatever!" He holds up his hands. "I'll show you. Wait here."

I do. I'm not about to go back and 'fess up to Madison about the Santa music. Besides, what Colby is offering is pretty great. At home, Dani and some of my other friends and I used to do the Christmas scavenger hunts together, and this feels a little bit closer to the way it should be.

Colby soon returns with a full smile. "I just talked with Miles. He's okay with us going to the piazza now and then meeting up with the others when they're done here. We've got one hour."

"And Madison?"

"I guess Miles will take care of that." He reaches out a hand and helps pull me to my feet. "Besides, the piazza is not far at all."

"Wow. Thanks." I awkwardly grab my now-broken backpack and follow him through the crowds and outside. The fresh air is nice, especially after all the sleepy fatigue of gallery after gallery.

As if he's been doing it all his life, Colby hails a cab and starts talking to the driver in broken Italian, and soon we are zipping around the crowded roundabouts. It all feels a bit more chaotic in a car instead of our high-up bus. The driver likes to use his horn, and I can hardly believe how we squeeze through some tiny alleys. But somehow, after a short but breathless ride, we make it in one piece.

I pull out some euros and then try to do the math on a tip.

"Use these," Colby says, fishing out a purple, yellow, and orangish bill, which I hand to the smiling cab driver. He leaves, and I turn around to see the piazza stretching before me. It's wide open, an ancient meeting place that the elegant old buildings have peered down on for centuries. Today its perimeter is crowded with people—workers on lunch break, tourists snapping pictures, and lots and lots of pigeons. In the middle, small wooden houses are set up in several rows for what looks like a holiday market.

As we walk down the rows, I'm reminded of the Christkindlmarket back in Chicago. Artisans have their wares set out for shoppers to browse: handmade jewelry, wood carvings, art, little toys. I make a mental note to see about coming back here to do some Christmas shopping later, but as we approach the end of the market stalls and the open part of the square, I start to feel funny. My breath is coming in too-short gasps and everything around me is threatening to tilt and spin. Usually I get amped about a scavenger hunt and dive right in, but now, for the first time ever with a hunt, I'm wondering what might go wrong. What if I trip and fall right now? What if I pass out unexpectedly? What if Madison is right and

I'm just being a stupid American?

Over on the other side of the piazza, a group of musicians is stationed near a café. Cello and violin and flute blend together to make lovely music that carries across the crisp winter air.

"See?" Colby says, pointing at them. "There's your dancing opportunity."

"I don't see any dancing," I say flatly.

"Well, at night, there's dancing."

A lot of good that does me. It's not night. And no one else is even close to dancing. A few listeners have gathered around the musicians—a friendly-looking older couple, a family with twin toddlers, and a cluster of people that must be part of a tour group. I take comfort from the fact that none of them look mean. One of the toddlers is even jerking up and down in what could technically pass for a dance. The older couple think it's cute.

Awesome. Thanks, Dad, I think as I realize I'm about to be dancing right next to a toddler. The older couple might not think it's so cute when a thirteen-year-old starts to groove.

I move a little closer, and all of a sudden, a horde of pigeons swoop down and land on some poor innocent man who's sitting closer to the café. I look around to see if anyone is going to help him.

"This guy is great," Colby says, unperturbed, and I follow Colby over to see what he means. Somehow the man is totally cool with the bird attack. He lies down flat on his back on the stone ground. He sprinkles crumbs of crackers and bread all over his black clothing, and the pigeons go absolutely nuts. Soon, he's covered in birds, their dark wings noisy as they push and jostle for the best crumbs.

"Why would—" I start. "I mean, just . . . why?"

Colby shrugs. "Why not? He's been here every year I've visited. I think it's performance art or something. Dude must like birds."

"I guess." It's kind of gross, especially when one of the birds poops on his jeans, but the more I watch the more fascinating I find it. The pigeon man doesn't seem to care what other people think at all. He's just doing his thing, however weird. And a lot, I mean *a lot*, more could go wrong with his thing than could go wrong with my dancing.

The crowd around us is shifting, drawing closer to the pigeon man now that the musicians have reached a pause in their set, and I make my way over to them. First, I find out if anyone speaks English. Fortunately they all do.

"Your music is beautiful," I say. "Do you mind if I dance

a little when you start playing again?"

The woman with the cello looks pleased. "But of course! Music and dancing are like brother and sister. What shall I play for you?"

"Something Christmassy?" I say, feeling some of my old nervousness return.

"*Bellissimo*," the violinist says. "'Gesù Bambino.' One of the most famous of Italian Christmas carols."

As soon as the musicians begin to play, people drift in our direction, but I try to block them out.

"Take a picture," I order Colby, slapping my phone into his hand. If I'm going to do this for real, I need proof to send Dad afterward.

At first, the music is really hard to get into, especially because dancing alone is kind of awkward. Okay, really awkward. I float around the edges of the musicians a bit, linger near the scattering pigeons, and then send them flying upward as I coast by. I close my eyes and try to find the rhythm. I'm not the best dancer. I've taken a few years of ballet, which really doesn't count anymore since all I can remember are the feet positions, but I'm amazed at how good it feels to focus on the music and just let it wash over me. As the song comes to an end, I open my eyes and see that all of my worry is for nothing. No one's even really been watching me at all. Except the cellist, who catches my eye with a wink and launches into a lively rendition of "Jingle Bells."

Now that I'm warmed up, I don't care what anyone else thinks. The bouncing toddler is back, and his dad puts him up on his shoulders, bobbing to the tune, and other people are swaying or singing along. I grab Colby's elbow, tugging him toward the music.

"Put that down." I point to my broken backpack, which he's been holding. "No, wait. Even better." I grab tacky dancing Santa and situate him for a good view, then hook my arm through Colby's as if we're square dancing.

"Wait a sec," he says, dragging his feet. "I didn't sign up for the dancing part."

"Oh, come on. Live a little." I pull him along after me. "Who doesn't like square dancing?"

"Um, me?" he says, but he's laughing as I switch arms and tug us the other direction. The older couple is back, and they join us, too, weaving in and out, along with the pigeon man, who jumps in with his own rendition of the chicken dance.

All too soon the song is over, and I spin Colby around for one last whirl. If we hadn't been on our way to being friends before, we would be now. You can't dance with someone in front of strangers without bonding or something. And it's that way with the other people as well.

Everyone is a little breathless and rosy-cheeked as we scatter with waves and holiday wishes.

After we take a few photos with the musicians, making sure tacky Santa is posed just right, Colby says we'd better go. "The group is meeting for a snack around three. That's when I told Miles we'd be back." We thank the musicians again and say good-bye, heading for the curbside, where this time I try—and succeed in!—hailing a cab. During the ride, I text Dani and my dad the photos. I know Dani is up early because today she has music lessons before school.

I KNEW you would have fun! she texts back. **I'm so jelly. And who is that hottie you're dancing with? Details! Now!**

I feel my cheeks grow warm and glance over at Colby, who is practicing his Italian with the cab driver. I feel relieved that there's no way he could have possibly seen what Dani texted, but it's still embarrassing.

Colby's a friend, I text back. **That's all. He's helping me with this crazy dare-scavenger hunt thing Dad planned for me.**

Right, Dani texts back with a few kissy emojis. She's almost as bad as Kylie.

Gotta run, I text as the cab pulls up in front of the curb. **More later.**

The others are where Miles said they would be—waiting at the benches in the foyer of the Galleria. Colby and I join right in, and it's hard to say if any of them even noticed we were gone. After everyone arrives, we all file outside to a pizza stand around the corner. When it's my turn, I'm tempted for the tiniest moment to be crazy and order a special pizza. The unexpected *has* been pretty fun. But I chicken out when I consider how it would totally be a downer to end the dare with spontaneous anaphylaxis, so I go for my usual cheese.

When it's ready, I take my pizza and join the other girls, who are perched on the steps of an old fountain. Sasha is talking to Kylie about what they saw in the museum. "Did you see the details on those vases and ceramics? I can't believe they did that with rudimentary tools."

Kylie is nodding in a distracted way, her attention more on the boys, who are sitting on some nearby steps.

"I know, right?" I plop down next to Sasha. I'm glad to discover a kindred art lover in Sasha. I told her about the effect the statues had on me. "It must be so fulfilling to make something like that, something that will last for centuries." I see that she has a sketch pad out and has created some cool geometric patterns.

She notices me looking. "I'm trying to work out some

of those designs to see if I can use them on my stuff."

"What kind of stuff?"

"I like to do arts and crafts sorts of things. Mobiles. Ceramics. Decorative arts."

"They are *so* showing off." Kylie sounds kind of pleased. In front of her, Logan is teaching Colby and Owen how to handspring off the nearest stair railing.

"Hmm," I say noncommittally, then turn back to Sasha. "Can I see some more of your sketches?"

Sasha flips the page to one where she's been working on interwoven leaves and patterns that look totally lifelike.

"That's really good," Kylie says.

"Totally," I say. "I like how you make them seem to lift off the page. I'm really inspired by nature. Landscapes are my thing."

Sasha's face brightens. "Oh, like watercolors?"

"Yup. And sketching, too. Autumn in Chicago is incredible for nature studies."

We talk about the art classes we've taken and the kind of tools we like to use, and suddenly I realize that I feel kind of warm and happy inside. I'm surprised to look down and see that I've polished off my cheese pizza without even once wondering if something unknown fell into it during food prep or something. I'd say that's a win.

10

THE NEXT MORNING I'M AWAKE before the bellman taps on my door, and I make my way over while working the clasp on my favorite jingle-bell necklace. He's holding a long, shiny, metallic polka-dot box and has a hint of a grin.

"Wait." I take it from him. "Do you know my dad? I mean, Signor Vasile?"

"My lips are sealed," he says with a knowing smile, but I take that as confirmation that he must be in on the dares. I wonder how many people Dad has recruited for this ultimate scavenger hunt.

After closing the door, I open the package to find a costume made up of a broomstick, a gray wig, and an old-fashioned red shawl. I have no clue why Dad's sent me that, even after peering at the toymaker elf gift tag pinned to the fabric. #2: DARE YOU TO PLAY LA BEFANA AT THE PALAZZO STROZZI it says with a little smiley face. There's also a flyer for the palazzo, which from what I can tell seems like some kind of community center for neighborhood meetings, local artists, and cultural education. Dad has circled a few of today's main events—children's storytelling hours—and put a smiley face with a pointy hat by them. I'm not sure what that's supposed to mean, except that Dad really can't draw at all.

I grab the guidebook, a handful of granola bars, and a satchel to replace my broken backpack. Mom is sitting on the edge of her bed in the second stage of wake-up, coffee in one hand and makeup spread around her.

"Bye," I say from over near the door. "I hope today goes well."

"For you, too, sweetheart." She snaps a compact shut. "I can't wait to hear all about it. I promise we'll have more time together soon."

"It's okay," I say cheerfully, meaning it in more ways than one. The actors have been using every spare moment for rehearsals before opening night, which means that Mom and I rarely see each other. Which is fine by me. I've felt weird being around her ever since The Kiss. She's acting all normal and Mom-ish and everything, but it feels like there's some big *thing* between us, like an invisible brick wall. I could ask her about The Kiss, but she obviously doesn't want me to know about S.T., and if I'm honest, I'm not really sure I want to hear what she has to say. What if she's in love with S.T. or something?

"See you later," I say, opening the door. "Break a leg." I'm not sure how I'll get through the upcoming free days on our itinerary where we'll be spending all our time together, but for now, I'm glad to push the whole S.T.– Mom thing out of my mind.

In the lobby, I spot Colby sitting near the buffet. He waves me over, and on the way I grab a few pieces of safe-looking fruit to round out my granola bar breakfast.

"So?" he says once I'm settled. "Another dare today?"

I show him the note and flip open the guidebook and skim through the descriptions, reporting as I go. "It looks like Palazzo Strozzi used to be a fancy palace five hundred years ago. Now it's known for its architecture and the cultural events that regularly take place there." We read through the description a second time, but there's no mention of the Befana. I even check the index. *Nothing*.

Colby pulls out his phone and with a few clicks comes up with the answer. "Oh. No wonder. It looks like the Befana has nothing to do with the Palazzo Strozzi. She's a witch version of Santa Claus. Kind of?"

I grab the phone from him and read the article: "La

Befana flies through the sky on the twelfth night of Christmas, leaving cakes and cookies for children." I keep reading, and we learn that the twelfth night is actually twelve days after Christmas, but I'll be back in Chicago then. Dad's obviously decided that today is just as good as the twelfth day of Christmas for me to act ridiculous again. If this Befana is a witch, and I've got a witchy costume in the box, and there is a little stick-figure witch by the story hours, it's not that much of a mystery. Witches at story time is definitely part of the unexpected, but how hard can it be? At least it's not dancing in front of strangers again.

"I think I'm supposed to pretend to be this Befana person at one of these children's story times." I compare the itinerary with the guidebook's map, which shows the location of Palazzo Strozzi. "They're not that far. I guess we could easily walk from the cathedral." The Santa Maria Novella Church is our first stop, and I read up on it while Colby goes back to the buffet for seconds. I learn that the church is famous for its architectural history and its many impressive chapels.

Later, when we are actually there, I see that the guidebook doesn't even come close to doing it justice. It's got that same ancient, quiet feel inside that I noticed back at the cathedral with the crèches. I spend a long time sitting in front of a window that depicts the Virgin Mary holding

Baby Jesus. Someone has left a bunch of little candles in front of it, several of which are lit, and the stained-glass face looks almost alive in the flickering light. I'm not really a religious person. Sometimes we go to mass if my grandmother is in town, but usually we kind of do our own thing and hope everything turns out right with the universe and all that. But in a place like this, where the stillness lies thick and heavy on my shoulders, where people have come for thousands of years through all their disappointments and heartbreaks and joys, I feel like I could almost really pray. And if I did, there might be some Being out there that might listen.

For now, I decide that sitting still in the quiet is almost like praying anyway. I drop a coin in the little box by the window and light one of the candles, and even though I'm afraid I'll feel silly, I say a whispered "Thank you," for the beauty of the place, and a "Help!" for the whole S.T.-and-Mom thing and the anaphylaxis and the divorce and, well, everything.

When I sit back on the hard pew, it seems like some of the quiet has soaked into my skin. I stay there until Colby finds me.

"Miles says it's cool if we go now as long as we aren't gone too long."

I kind of don't want to leave. There's something special

about being hidden away inside such a peaceful place while the rest of the city races around outside. But an hour is only an hour, and a dare is a dare, so soon we are out in the bustle, too.

On the way to Palazzo Strozzi, we stop by a little gift shop that has a bathroom next to it. I've already discovered that you have to pay to use public restrooms here, so I take the costume with me and drop some coins in for the fee. As I put on the clothes, I get that nervous feeling again. I fiddle with the cape, wishing that it was all over and done with and I was on the way back from the dare rather than going *to* it.

What is wrong with me? Why am I afraid to go to toddler story time? "Pull it together," I tell myself in the mirror. I try on the wig, which definitely makes me look like an old lady, except with very young skin, ew, and decide to wait to wear it until I'm actually there. I smooth the fabric of the costume down and something crinkles in the pocket. I discover a little slip of paper with a poem about the Befana printed on it, all about how she comes to children and brings them presents. That would've been helpful to find earlier. I crumple it up and shove it back in my pocket. I splash water on my face to try to get the nervous feeling to go away, but it stays put.

I check my watch as I leave the bathroom. I have a few minutes to finish planning. I can get to the Palazzo Strozzi, but what am I supposed to do then? Put on my crazy wig and crash story time? I at least need some presents. I buy some Florentine biscuits in the shop so I have something to hand out, but when I'm done, Colby doesn't seem at all ready to go.

Already I can feel the nervousness ballooning inside at the thought of being too late to do the dare and thinking about anything else that might go wrong. "I thought we only had an hour," I say when I come up beside him. "We've got to hurry." My words come out all tight and bossy.

Colby spins around, showing me a bag of tiny wooden Pinocchio puppets. "For the kids," he says, holding one between his fingers to make it dance in midair.

"Oh, good idea!" I say, feeling guilty for being annoyed, and we hurry the rest of the way to the palazzo.

As we reach the door, I see that the same flyer Dad sent me is posted on the window. Right now, the lunchtime story hour is nearly over. As we enter the building I feel a burst of energy, like I'm über-caffeinated or something. I wonder what the people in there will think if I just bust in wearing a random costume. Will they kick us out? Will they think I'm crazy?

"So should I just go in there and hand things out?" I say, realizing that for all of my worrying, I don't actually have a plan.

"Why don't you ask her?" Colby says, pointing to a friendly-looking grandmotherly woman sitting at the front desk.

Oh, duh! Talking to someone in charge makes sense. If they say yes, then I'll at least have some sort of official approval to bolster my nerves. If they say no, well, they say no, and I'll still have tried the dare. But the lady behind the counter doesn't say no. Instead, she claps her hands together, and her face crinkles into a megawatt smile.

"What a beautiful idea!" she says in a thick accent. "I will explain to the storyteller that she should not send the children away just yet." I peer through the big window and see the eyes of the young woman who's reading books to the children grow wide when the grandma whispers in her ear. Then she launches into some announcement in enthusiastic Italian. The children start wiggling in their seats, looking around in anticipation, and there are even a few claps and cheers.

I guess that's my cue. "Here goes nothing," I say to Colby as I tug on the gray wig.

Colby hands me the bag of little puppets. "Good luck."

Entering the room is even harder than starting to dance. At least then, the musicians were also performing, so it wasn't just everyone's attention spotlighted on me. But now, believe me, I feel every single pair of eyes as I come in the room, and I realize I have no idea what to say. Will they even be able to understand me if I speak English? Should I have bothered to look up something, anything, to say in Italian?

I take a deep breath. Italian or not, there's no going back now. However ridiculous I seem, I am so not going to make a whole roomful of children cry by bailing on the dare. I've learned from Colby's quick search that the Befana is supposed to be hunting for the Christ child to give him gifts, so I pretend that I am looking hard for someone. I shade my eyes and peer toward the back of the room, straining my eyes and pulling my mouth down, which makes the children start to giggle. I stoop and act like I'm looking low down on the ground, as though something is hidden under the pretty rug on the floor. Then, when my path takes me to the first row of children, I clap my hands in delight and open the box of cookies, darting around the room handing them out to the children. I don't know if the Befana is supposed to say anything or not, but the children seem pleased enough, as happy sounds fill the room.

I watch them munch, feeling awkward. *Should I have done more?* As I move to the side of the room, my hand brushes against my pocket, and I remember the poem. I pull out the little crumpled paper and read it aloud, acting it out as I go:

Here comes, here comes the Befana
She comes from the mountains in the deep of the night
Look how tired she is! All wrapped up
In snow and frost and the north wind!
Here comes, here comes the Befana!

I pause every few lines for the storyteller to translate, and by the time we are done, I am smiling right along with the children. I make another loop, this time with the wooden puppets, and the children are even more excited about those. It's awesome to see how excited they all are by a cookie and a little toy.

The room fills with laughter as they try to work the puppets, and it kind of turns into chaos with, as far as I can tell, kids asking for seconds on cookies and some of the littlest kids chasing each other with their puppets. I guess that means it's been a success? As I turn to go, I notice one little girl hanging back from the mob of racing children, looking exactly how I felt a few minutes ago—

nervous, unsure, and a little afraid.

I take off my mask and wig and bend down to her level, beckoning her closer. "Do you want a toy, too?" I hold up a cute puppet wearing a painted red dress.

Her face lights up, and she inches forward to grab it with a whispered *"Grazie"* before rushing back to the safety of what I'm guessing is her grandfather's arms.

The caretakers begin to wrangle the children toward the door, some of them stopping to thank me in English or comment on my costume. As I follow the last few out, I realize that I've been so occupied with whether the kids are having a good time that I've kind of forgotten about all my nervousness. Which, I'm not going to lie, feels pretty spectacular. On the way to meet up with our tour group, I stop by the Pinocchio seller's stall and buy three puppets— one to give Dad for when I tell him about the dares, one for Dani, and one for me. I pick the same one I gave to the little girl.

"So. That was a big win," Colby says when I rejoin him with my bag.

"Not bad at all." I grin. "Thanks for helping me. The puppets were a great idea."

"Just doing my job," he says, but I can tell that he's pleased.

The good feeling doesn't last long, however. When we

arrive at the appointed meeting place, it isn't like yesterday, where everyone is just chilling and no one has noticed we were gone. Instead, the other kids are all staring at us with warning looks. Miles is standing to one side, his hands stuck in his pockets, purposely avoiding eye contact. And Madison is on a mission.

"I need to speak with you both," she says brusquely, pulling us a few paces away from the others. I can tell that this is not a Good Thing.

"You guys can't just go off like that," she says in this really serious voice. "Not least because this is a foreign city, and you are Americans who don't even speak the language. But also because your parents are trusting us to be in charge of you. Miles and I are supposed to look out for you and keep you safe." She wipes a hand across her forehead, and I wonder if under all her lecturing she might be a little bit worried. "Do you guys realize how serious this is? Something bad could have happened, or you could have needed help, and we had no idea where you were."

"I told Miles—" Colby begins, but Madison doesn't let him finish.

"What you told Miles was that you wouldn't be far and would meet us on the steps of the cathedral. You did not tell him you were going to race off to some other part of the city. There's a difference." She shoots Miles a glare that is wasted on him since he's now joking with the other kids.

"Oh." Colby looks down at his shoes.

"Look, I know you've traveled a lot, Colby, but you've still got to follow the rules, too. They are there to keep you safe. No more running off without telling anyone where you are going. Actually, no more running off, period. Everyone stays with the group."

I want to defend myself, but right now I feel silly and embarrassed and about five years old, and the dares just seem childish and stupid.

"Christa, I know your dad has some special activities planned for you, but I don't think he meant for you to sneak off and secretly do them, okay? I'll check back in with him, but from here on out, you stay with the group, too, okay?"

Phew! I'm glad I don't have to tell her about the dares. "I'm sorry," I tell her, my face hot with embarrassment. "I didn't mean to cause trouble."

I don't mind the rest of Madison's lecture much, because I can see her point. I just sort of assumed that since Dad was sending me the dares, I had permission to do whatever I needed to do. But I see now that it doesn't make a lot of sense. Of course Dad didn't mean for me to be wandering around Florence on my own. Even if both times we didn't go very far at all. But then it goes way beyond a lecture. Madison calls the whole group together to talk about

Group Safety and how important it is for us all to Be Alert and Stay Together. She's talking to all of us, but clearly Colby and I are responsible for this wave of reprimand.

I can feel the others staring at us, but I just keep my eyes fixed on the toes of my boots. I do look up when Madison pulls out a big bag from the cathedral gift shop and takes out a handful of bright neon-yellow visors.

"These will make it easier for us to keep track of you," she says, passing them out. "When we are on tour, you need to wear them."

No one bothers to muffle their groans. The visors are beyond ugly. Not to mention embarrassingly attention-drawing.

"Seriously?" Kylie gives me and Colby a poisonous look. "Maddie"—which is what she calls Madison now—"we don't need these. At all."

For once I totally agree with Kylie, but I keep my mouth shut. I've gotten into enough trouble as it is. Besides, it's because of me that everyone has to look ridiculous.

"Better safe than sorry," Madison says, cramming one down on her head.

I exchange glances with Colby, who looks sheepish. "Sorry," he says. "I didn't know they'd be so upset."

"It's as much my fault as yours," I say, trying to resign myself to the ugliness of the hat. It's no worse than the gray wig, but I wish I could somehow take it all back and do the dares differently. Madison leads the way to the bus, and Miles walks up next to us. Somehow he makes the visor look cool.

"Don't worry," he says. "She'll chill in a few days." He looks at Colby. "But you should've told me exactly where you'd be, bro. Next time, okay?" And they do a fist bump. Miles offers me one, too, but even Miles's reassurance can't overcome the silliness I feel, especially when I Velcro (Velcro!) the yellow visor onto my forehead.

11

THE NEXT MORNING IS THE first one that I don't meet up with M&M's tour group. The actors are done with rehearsals for now, since performances in Florence have started. Which means that today I'm going to have to deal with Mom. I putter about the suite, munching on one of my granola bars and setting out my clothes for the day. Ugly Christmas sweater, check. Today's has wicked-looking elves working away on children's toys. Dark green jeans that look better than they sound, check. And candy-cane earrings, of course.

The morning's knock on the door brings me a gift bag with a velvet box containing a silver necklace with a heart strung on it. As I look closer, I see that the heart has a small keyhole. A tiny old-fashioned-looking key is attached to the snowflake gift tag, which reads: #3: DARE YOU TO FIND THE MATCHING PADLOCK AT THE PONTE VECCHIO. I plop onto my bed and flip through the guidebook. It turns out the bridge is a famous spot for lovers to come and lock up their hearts before throwing away the key. It's a little too mushy for me, especially when I think of how complicated relationships can get. I mean, I know that my parents locked up their hearts a few years ago on an anniversary trip they took to Italy. So what are divorced people supposed to do? Come back and *unlock* their hearts? Add an additional little lock with Mom and S.T.'s initials? I toss the book to the end of the bed. This dare doesn't make me nervous—just annoyed. Besides, hasn't Dad thought about how awkward this is going to be to do around Mom? Yesterday, Europe was all stars and wonder and ancient cathedrals, and today I want to hole up in my hotel room and avoid seeing everyone.

Later, at breakfast, I'm eating some cornflakes—the hotel put out some frosted ones for the win—and listening to Mom rave about how wonderful the play is.

"I'm so glad Madison has all you kids coming to see the performance tonight," she says, poking at a half grapefruit. "Nic has added so many little touches that make everything extra Christmassy."

I mumble a "Great," but inside I'm feeling anything but. Now that Mom is actually sitting across the table from me, I realize I'm still fuming inside about how she's kept the whole S.T. thing from me. Not to mention how it means she's totally over her marriage to Dad in, like, a month and a half or whatever. And I know it's kind of bratty to complain about being in Europe and everything, but come on! If it wasn't for Mom's "big chance," I'd be at home with Dad rocking all the fun Christmassy things instead of being That Kid on the tour who is responsible for ruining everyone else's photos forever with horrible yellow visors. All of that combined makes me want to absolutely not be pretending to cheer Mom on at her play tonight. Plus, if I'm really honest, there's another reason I don't want to go. This is going to be my first time going to one of Mom's plays without Dad, and that feels super weird and final. Like things really are *that* different.

Mom's phone buzzes, and she stops talking to check it out. "Oh no!" she says, texting back. "Chris, I can't believe this! I know it's our first free day together, but Nic has called me and Sandra in for an extra tech rehearsal with the understudy. Cami's sick. Food poisoning, I guess."

I poke my spoon into my soggy cereal. There's no bacteria hiding in there with all the fortified vitamins and sugar, right?

Mom looks up at me, her face crinkled with concern. "Will you be mad if I have to bail on today's plans? Maybe I could tell Nic I can't do it until this afternoon." She starts texting. "No. This is silly. I'm going to tell him *no*. The show will be fine. I'm not going to miss my only day in Florence with my daughter."

"Mom." I grab her wrist. "It's fine. We'll have lots of time together later. And then a whole day in Paris, right? And London, too?" I don't tell her how relieved I feel at this unexpected twist. If we spend all day alone together she's sure to notice something's wrong, and I really, really, *really* don't want to talk about her and S.T. and the whole play without Dad thing and all the feelings. Besides, it will be so much easier to complete today's dare without her.

"Are you sure?"

"Totally," I say. "Look. This is your once-in-a-lifetime opportunity to do a European tour. You should go. I'll be fine."

She hesitates, but only for a moment. "Okay. But I'm telling him that this is it. No more unplanned rehearsals." She texts back an answer, and I let my gaze wander around the room over the other guests. Colby comes in and waves at me from the espresso bar.

"Besides," I say, the spark of an idea forming. "Colby and I can do some sightseeing. He's been to Florence loads of times and even speaks Italian."

"Um, no," Mom says, setting her phone down. "Two thirteen-year-olds alone in a European city? No way." She leans in, her phone forgotten. "Madison told me what happened. I was waiting to talk to you about it until we were alone today. Chris, you can't just go wandering around on your own. This isn't Oak Park." Mom goes on to say that I'm only allowed to be on my own in the hotel lobby or our suite. Otherwise, I have to be with a "responsible adult" at all times. She reaches for her cell again. "Maybe this is a bad idea after all. It's not fair that you should have to hole up here while I work."

S.T. walks up to our table with a big smile. "Why should anyone have to stay in the hotel on such a beautiful morning in Italy?" Okay, I take back what I said earlier. I now have found the one theater guy who actually *is* a morning person.

He does a silly little bow. "It's our day off, Jocelyn. Put the phone away. Come explore the magic of Italy with me."

I try not to gag. *The magic of Italy? With him?*

Kylie is right behind her dad, and she plops down next to me with a plate of salami and fruit. "Hey, Christa. What's up?"

"Mmm," I grunt. "Too early."

Mom fills S.T. in on her extra rehearsal, and while Kylie chats with me about how wonderful the hotel water pressure is, I am horrified to hear Todd offer to take me sightseeing along with him and Kylie. And, before I can say anything, Mom is actually agreeing!

"Oh, Todd, you're such a lifesaver!" Mom turns to me with a big smile. "Did you hear that?"

I wish I hadn't. Short of pretending to spontaneously come down with the flu, I can't speed-think a way out of this. Kylie is already practically jumping up and down in her chair, if that's possible.

"What about Colby?" I ask, scrambling for something to make this somewhat tolerable. "If you're at rehearsal with Nic, won't he be stuck at the hotel, too? Maybe I should stay here and keep him company."

"Oh, let's have him come, too, Dad!" Kylie's chair is seriously scooting around in her excitement.

"The more the merrier," S.T. says cheerfully, and then smugly side-hugs Mom. *Barf.*

In a matter of minutes, it's all settled. I find myself agreeing to meet them in the lobby in fifteen minutes, and Kylie rushes over to Colby. I watch him nod, look back at me and shrug, and nod again. I sigh, tossing my napkin alongside my bowl of abandoned cornflakes. At least it won't be horrible with Colby along. Maybe with our powers combined we can figure out a way to complete the dare without having to tell Kylie and S.T. about it. I shiver as I imagine the scenario where Kylie is narrating how romantic the whole padlocked bridge is. *Nope.* That's not going to happen. My mini vision continues with S.T. examining a heart lock and then getting all swoony-eyes about him and Mom on it. *Double barf.*

"Oh, I'm glad this is working out so perfectly!" Mom says, happily returning to her grapefruit.

"Mmm," I say, thinking about how wildly different people's ideas of perfection can be.

"And then you and I will get Girl Time this afternoon!" Mom says. "I'm *dying* to see the Boboli Garden."

"I've already seen it," I say flatly, frustrated at myself that I didn't speak up and say no sooner. What was I thinking? A whole morning with S.T.? Pretending to be sick would be so much better than this.

Mom is giving me a funny look. "Well, maybe you can show me your favorite spots in it, then. I'd love to hear what you think about everything you've seen so far."

Ha! If she only knew all that I've seen.

I stand, grabbing my bag. "Maybe Todd can take you. I'm sure you'll have a great time together." I ignore the confused look on Mom's face. "Whatever. Look, I've got to get ready to meet the others. See you later, okay?"

I don't really need to get anything, but I do *really* need a break from Mom and everything before I get snarky and mean. I love Mom. I know her play is important. I'm happy for her. But, seriously, it's like she's dialed in to the Mom-only planet.

Colby and I spend a few hours wandering around with S.T. and Kylie, and though I really hate to say it, it's not awful. S.T. and Kylie are not horrible people. There, I said it. They're actually kind of nice, which is frustrating, because I really want S.T. to be a jerk. Instead, he and Kylie are like the annoying friends on a sitcom. They are extraordinarily cheerful, excited about everything, and full of energy. And I actually like that S.T. doesn't make us do anything specific. No itineraries for him. We walk around, stop for chocolate, people-watch, and feed the pigeons. S.T. also has some interesting stories to tell since he's toured through Europe a lot.

In fact, the morning might actually have been fun if Kylie hadn't spent most of it flirting with Colby. Seriously. She couldn't pass any postcard stand or gelato shop without an "Ohmigosh, Colby!" and a giggle. And then, of course, remembering that however cool S.T. seems, he secretly made out with Mom, which obviously puts a whole damper on the fun factor. *Ew.*

All things considered, I'm pretty relieved when S.T. says it's almost time to head back to the hotel. First, though, he takes us souvenir shopping on the Ponte Vecchio, an arched walkway that stretches across the Arno River. The first and last parts of the bridge are partly enclosed with shops on each side and rows of festive evergreen branches overhead. From where we stand outside a shop that sells purses, I can see the open center area where the padlocks are supposed to be. I decide that now is my best shot at trying to complete the dare without having to tell S.T. and Kylie about it all.

"Is it okay if Colby and I wait up there for you guys?" I cross my fingers that this will work. "We won't do any exploring. I just want to look at the padlocked hearts." And it's the truth. I *won't* explore anything else.

"I think that's okay," S.T. says, considering. "We'll just be at those shops over there, so as long as we can see you when we come out, that sounds good to me."

"Come on, Dad." Kylie is tugging S.T. toward a jewelry shop.

S.T. looks at his watch. "Give us thirty minutes."

After they're gone, I fill Colby in on the dare. He looks a bit doubtful.

"Do you know how many hearts there are? This could take all day."

"It better not. We only have half an hour." The last people I want helping me find my parents' heart lock is S.T. and Kylie. "Besides, Dad drew a little map." I pull out the note that came with the dare. "We don't have to search through them all."

Without the map, there's no way we could have found it. Thousands of padlocks in every size and color are hooked on the bridge, the railing, the posts, even down below on the bridge supports. Tourists crowd around, snapping selfies, and locals frown down on what has become a famous landmark. A few policemen linger nearby, and I'm betting that they're there to catch anyone trying to put a lock on. The guidebook told me that now people get fined for doing it.

Honestly, I totally get why. It is seriously like someone has constructed a fence out of metal locks. I guess it's romantic, but to me, it's also kind of ugly. Fortunately, my parents' lock is in a less popular part of the bridge, probably because it's from a few years ago. Tucked in the middle of a rusty jumble that smells like metal, their old lock looks exactly like the one that came in the box this morning, except that it's been worn down by the elements. Which, not so subtly, feels representative of my parents' marriage.

I take my sleeve and rub off some of the grime. Their initials, A.V. & J.V., are carved above the keyhole . . . and below them, my name. I wonder what they felt like when they knelt here to fasten the lock. Did they ever imagine that their love wouldn't last?

"Are you okay?" Colby asks from my elbow. I almost forgot he's there and am embarrassed that he's caught me starting to cry. I scrub at my eyes.

"I'm fine. I just don't get why Dad would dare me to look at this." I let the heart drop with a clang. "Their love didn't last forever. And now I might as well scribble out Dad's initials and carve in a big fat S.T. instead." I wad up the note my dad sent and throw it in the trash. "It's a stupid tradition. All of these people thinking their love is never going to change." Close by us a young couple is posing with their lock. After they snap the photo, they look around to make sure the policemen aren't watching and then kneel to hook it on together.

"Like them. How long will it last? A year or two? Three years ago my parents were so sure they were in love, and now? Now we don't even spend Christmas together. *Christmas!* When families should be together to do All the Christmas Things." The candy-cane earrings snag on my hair as I gesture, and I feel like tearing them off. It doesn't matter how many ugly Christmas sweaters I've packed or how much fun holiday jewelry I wear or how much of the scavenger hunt I complete, I can't transport my back-home Christmas to Europe. What we used to have is over. Christmas, and probably every other family holiday, will never be the same again. I spy S.T. taking a picture of Kylie over by the scarf shop. "*And* my mom has already moved on. I can't believe she totally didn't care that she broke up our family."

"Well, she didn't completely break you up," Colby says in a quiet voice. "She's here with you, isn't she? And didn't you say your parents are still friends? Maybe that's why your dad wanted you to see the lock. To show that there's still some way for you all to be together."

A part of me knows that Colby might be right, but the other part of me, the one that's pissed, tells that first part to shut up.

"Besides," Colby continues, "if they both thought a divorce would be best for them, maybe it is."

"What's best for them. Whatever that means." As I talk, I realize that I've spent the last weeks pretending like I'm okay with everything. I mean, I knew pretty early on that there wasn't a chance of Mom and Dad changing their minds or something, and the last thing I wanted was another conversation like the one we had on November first. So instead I tried to get excited about picking out stuff for my new room at Mom's and acted like it was a bonus to decorate two places for Christmas (okay, so that sort of was a win), and pretended that a movie marathon was just as fun with one parent as it is with two. I did everything I thought I was supposed to do to be like the girls in movies who seem totally chill about living with just one parent. Or the kids in my class whose parents have been divorced forever and seem not to even care. But the thing is, I do care. And I'm so not chill about it.

"Actually," I say bitterly, "I bet this *is* all Mom's fault. *She's* the one who moved out. *She's* the one who wanted something DIFFERENT for Christmas. *She's* the one who dragged me here. *She's* the one with the new apartment and new life. *She's* the one cheating on my dad. And *she's* the stupid reason I'm hanging out with S.T." I suck in a breath as I think of what that might mean. I mean, really mean, that there might be more to this than just a make-out party. "Ohmigosh, what if they're serious? What if Mom wants me to get to know him? Like S.T. as a"—I whisper the word—"stepfather?" I grab Colby's arm. "Oh no. This is bad. So bad. So much worse than I thought."

"Whoa," says Colby. "That's a lot to process."

Which is such an understatement. And in the worst possible timing, Kylie and S.T. are done shopping and heading toward us with cheerful smiles. Kylie wants to show me everything she bought, but I can barely manage a nod and an "Oh! Nice!" All I can think of is the word *stepsister* flashing like a neon sign over her head.

S.T. says he'll buy everyone a hot cocoa, but I can't even choke down a single sip.

"Christa is *so* moody," Kylie says in a not-quiet whisper to her dad as we leave the café. I know she's right. I'm being difficult and everyone can tell, but *I can't help it!* This is the worst possible Christmas surprise ever!

Colby tries to keep the mood light by talking about the time he was in Florence and rented a Vespa with his dad, but they got lost and ended up in some tiny village where no one spoke English. Kylie giggles at all the right places, but I feel like a robot, trying to smile and nod and not fall apart right there on the sidewalk.

Finally, S.T. puts me out of my misery by saying that we should probably head back to the hotel for lunch.

"Thanks," I say. "I'm not feeling very well." Which, despite my thoughts of fake-sicking it this morning, is *so* the truth right now. I feel awful.

At the hotel, I call room service, order a plain

hamburger, and eat it to my favorite Christmas playlist. I send Dani a monster text about the day: how S.T. took me sightseeing, my suspicions about his potential as stepfather material, and the awkwardness between me and Mom. She doesn't reply. When Madison calls up with a reminder about meeting to go see tonight's play performance, I tell her truthfully that I'm sick. There's no way I can hang out with other kids right now and watch Mom and S.T. onstage. When I hang up with Madison, I text Mom, who, of course, doesn't answer since she's getting ready to perform.

I order more room service and find a dubbed version of *It's a Wonderful Life* on TV, which doesn't really make me feel any better. Mom, Dad, and I used to watch it every Christmas Eve, but this year it doesn't have its usual charm. When the movie ends, I'm still left in a suite alone with the pieces of my not-so-wonderful life scattered around me.

My phone bings with a text. **Are you okay, Chris?** It's Mom. The play must be over.

Is it food poisoning? Cami said she thought she got sick from the hotel sausage.

Like I would eat sausage with unknown ingredients. **I'm a little better**, I text back. **Sorry I had to miss opening night. How did it go?**

As good as it could without you. Mom adds a bunch of heart emojis. **Get some rest, honey. I'll be back in an hour or so. I'll creep in so I don't wake you.** This is followed by a string of sleepy emojis.

The play must have gone really well. When I'm finished replying to Mom, I see that Dani has responded to my texts.

Juicy, she writes. **Your life is so fabulous. Europe. Stepparents. Drama. I miss you.**

I miss you, too. I turn my phone off. It's easy for Dani to say that as someone whose parents have been divorced since she was a baby. Divorce is her normal. It's not mine. And, I think as I fall asleep, it is definitely anything but fabulous.

12

IN THE MORNING, I WAIT a long time for the bell-man's tap on the door, but it never comes. Finally, I grab my things and get ready. I've been surprised at how festive the Christmas decorations on all the Florentine streets and shopfronts have been, but you can never have too much Christmas, right? I pull out my loudest and ugliest Christmas sweater, the one with Santa cats sleigh-riding all over it, and fasten my string-of-Christmas-lights anklet. It's our last day in Florence, and it's another free day. Which means I have to spend the whole time with Mom, either pretending everything is normal and fuming inside or somehow having to talk about S.T.

Outside the suite in the hall I see that there's a package waiting for me. *How did I miss the knock?* It's lightweight, and I bring it back inside and, ignoring all my present-opening rules, tear at it in a hurry. Inside, there is some kind of toy that looks like a cross between a slingshot and a flashlight. The gift tag is crisscrossed with strings of Christmas lights and reads #4: DARE YOU TO CLIMB THE PIAZZA DEL DUOMO'S BELL TOWER, and there's a little printed note with instructions telling me to go at five p.m. But neither of these gives me any clues as to what the gadget is.

Munching on a granola bar, I look up the Piazza del Duomo in the guidebook. I see that I've been there before. It houses the Florence Cathedral and a bunch of other famous buildings, but there's nothing related to the weird toy in the box. Unless climbing 414 stairs to the bell tower requires a toy. I check the itinerary. There's an optional kids' outing tonight, which looks like it's going to be my best shot for completing the dare, and a girls-only slumber party planned for afterward. I don't really like the sound of the slumber party, but who knows? I might be dying for it after a day with Mom. Just then, she comes out of the bathroom in her lounging clothes with a turban around her wet hair.

"Are you feeling better, Christa?"

I shove Dad's package under the covers. The dares

aren't a secret, but I somehow feel that Mom knowing about them will make it all really silly. I'm too slow.

"Is that from your dad?" Mom says in a careful voice, padding over to open the blinds. "I know he has a bunch of surprises planned for you. You two were always into your surprises." The words sound like they should be nice, but I know from the way she says them that she's annoyed at Dad. And at me for doing the dares with Dad. Which makes *me* super annoyed. Why does she care what I do with Dad? It's not like she has any say in his life anymore.

"Oh. So you've talked to Dad?" I say, perfectly calm. "I thought you might be too busy with *other people* to think about him."

Mom looks up from her pot of face cream, startled. "I *knew* I shouldn't have done the last-minute rehearsal yesterday. I'm sorry, Chris."

"Whatever," I mumble, deciding to let her think I'm upset about that. I don't really want to be the one to bring up S.T. What I want is for *her* to care enough to tell me. No, scratch that. What I really want is for none of this to ever have happened and for my parents to realize they've made a huge mistake and for Dad to fly out and for us to do Christmas together the Right Way.

A sharp knock on the door saves me from more

conversation. It's my favorite bellman, but this time he has a delivery for Mom—a beautiful arrangement of roses. Mom hands the bellman a euro coin, and I realize I probably should have been tipping him all along. Maybe that's why my package was just set outside today. *Oops.*

Mom shuts the door, chuckling over the note on the little tag, and I escape to the bathroom. Ugh. Who else but S.T. would send flowers? The morning has just gone from bad to worse.

When I come out, I don't have to lie about feeling sick again. My stomach is all in knots. "Maybe I don't feel well after all."

Mom feels my forehead. "You don't have a fever, hon," she says. "But I'm worried about you."

"I think I ate something bad," I say, remembering the suspicious spices on my french fries last night. If I'm lucky, Mom will see that I'm too sick to go shopping with her today, but not so sick that I can't stay in the hotel alone. "It's just a stomachache. I think I'll feel better if I stay here and rest. Near the . . . you know." I dart a glance at the bathroom.

"Oh, but that's the worst timing ever!" Mom reaches for the hotel guide. "Maybe there's a pharmacy or something close by. I don't want you to miss out on Europe because of an upset stomach. Let's see—"

"Look. It's no big deal. I ate something weird, and besides, I'm super tired, too, okay? I've seen a ton of Florence, and every day has been jam-packed while you've been at rehearsal. I only need to rest is all."

Mom drops the guide and holds up her hands in surrender. It's the most annoying thing ever, because she always does this when she claims I'm being too "sensitive."

"Fine," she says, toweling off her hair and sweeping it into a loose knot. "You get your rest. It sounds like you really need it." She grabs her bag. "I'll be back after lunch to change for the matinee performance. There's a special dinner to celebrate our Italian run afterward. I hope you'll feel well enough to come to one of those."

Mom's voice is all cool and collected, but I can tell she's annoyed. *Too bad.* There's no way I'm going to sit there and watch her and S.T. together onstage. And I definitely don't want a repeat of seeing them together at another cast party.

"Tonight?" I say in a sad voice. "Oh, that *is* terrible timing. There's a kids' outing that I was really hoping to go on planned for tonight." That's an exaggeration, but I'm suddenly feeling extra motivated not to be in the suite when Mom gets back. "And a girls' slumber party afterward." I shrug. "I guess they overbooked the itinerary."

Mom doesn't say anything. Just gives me one of those looks, the kind that make me want to squirm. I force out a weak cough. "I mean, if I feel well enough."

"Fine," Mom says. "Do what you want, Christa. You always do." She slips on her sunglasses and a forced smile. "After all, it's your trip, too."

Double ugh. I hate it when she gets all quiet like that. I know that whatever she says, it's not fine. Nothing about this is fine, especially the way I feel when I think of her last look.

I flip on the TV and scroll through the channels, hoping for something to get my mind off the sick-guilty feeling squirming its way through my insides. When I've nearly lost hope, I finally find that *Elf* is on. Perfect. Nothing like a little Christmas magic to make a day better. During the commercial breaks I wander around the suite getting snacks and coffee.

Once, I stop by the flowers, which Mom has set up on her nightstand. The little tag reads: *Proud of you. Break a leg, Joss.*

Ugh. S.T. is even stealing my dad's nickname for her. What a jerk. I decide to do a little more snooping. Mom's tote bag has crumpled scripts and crumbs from snacks and her stash of *People* magazines. Nothing from S.T. there. I do find some old travel brochures from Dad's office that Mom has marked with things to see and do. *Chris would love this,* she's written next to an article on the fashion district in Paris. Guiltily, I shove all the papers back in and try to remember that I'm mad at Mom.

After *Elf* comes some dubbed version of an old American sitcom that I can kind of follow, and then another showing of *Elf.* By that time it's late afternoon, and I debate whether I should keep hiding in the hotel and skip out on tonight's M&M outing, but I know that will only get me in more trouble with Mom. Besides, I'm feeling a bit stir-crazy, and of course, there's still the dare I need to do. I splash water on my face, comb my hair, and head to the lobby hoping that I can convince everyone to stop by the bell tower on the way. It turns out I don't even need to do that. M&M have planned an outing to take us all back to the Piazza del Duomo.

"Your dad's right," Colby says mysteriously when I show him the toy and tell him about the dare. "You'll know what to do when we get there." I'm not really in the mood for playfulness, so I hang with Sasha, who is walking behind the others, earbuds in. We walk together while Kylie links arms with Logan and Owen and they stagger along singing a really, really obnoxious version of "Rudolph, the Red-Nosed Reindeer."

Colby drops back to join me and Sasha. "Did you have a good day today? With your mom and everything?"

It's hard to ignore Colby when he's being sweet. "Not so good," I say. I tell him about the opposite-of-awesome moment we had this morning. "I get that she has her own life and everything, but I still think it's crazy that she already has another relationship. And a secret one!"

Colby is quiet for a little bit. Then he clears his throat awkwardly. "You're really lucky to have two parents who care about you, Christa." He's looking up into the sky as he talks. "I never see my mom. Like, ever."

I don't know what to say. I want to ask why he doesn't see her, but I don't know if that's okay or not. "That sucks," I say instead. I feel really stupid. I've been going off about Mom, and Colby doesn't even have a mom who is in his life. I know he's right. And I'm not wishing Mom away or anything. I just wish she were, well, different. "I'm sorry about your mom," I tell Colby, wondering what it would be like to have no mom around at all.

"I'm used to it."

We walk in silence, because there's not a whole lot to say. As we near the piazza, Sasha takes out her earbuds, which breaks the intensity of our conversation.

"What *is* that?" She points at the little flowers of light that are popping up in the air before us.

Colby grins. "I told you you'd know what the note meant when you got here."

"What note?" Sasha says, but instead of answering, I pull out the toy that came with the dare.

"My dad sent me this. I think they're for shooting those lights up somehow." I look back at the piazza and for a moment forget all about the dare. There, lit up in full holiday glory, is the gigantic Christmas tree we saw earlier. It stretches up against the pale walls of the cathedral toward the purpling sky in a brilliant blaze of light and color. That is more like it, Florence. That is the makings of a Christmas extravaganza.

When we finally arrive, M&M hand out the devices to everyone. They are little slingshots specially designed to fire LED lights. But it's super tricky to do. Logan gets the hang of it pretty quickly and tries to teach everyone else. Kylie almost dies laughing when she fires hers straight down to the ground, and she begs Logan to tell her what to do. Owen flanks her, and I can't tell if she's really having that hard of a time or just pretending.

Sasha gets hers going pretty soon, and Colby looks like

he's already done this before. I'm having trouble. Whenever I go to pull the little rubber band, the missile drops out. Finally, I get it to work. You have to put the right amount of pressure on the slingshot so it can give the light some height. But once you do, it's amazing, and the spark flares up to join all the others that are dancing around the piazza. It's pretty easy to find when it comes down, too, and we all just keep firing them, one after the other, to join in with the whole crazy display. The piazza looks as though the night air is filled with a thousand fireflies. After a while, M&M herd us all over to a gelato shop, where I order my usual vanilla.

Sasha and I sit together and talk. It turns out that besides art and drawing, she's really into horses and has two at home.

"Do you ride?" I ask her.

"A little," she says. "But I also draw them." She pulls out her sketch pad and shyly shows me a few drawings. "This is Misty. She's mine."

"Wow! Those are really good." And I'm not making it up. The sketch of Misty looks like a professional drawing of a horse.

"Thanks. What do you like to do for nature studies?"

I think of how I used to be all about sketching. "My

neighborhood, mostly." I've kind of stalled out on sketching, I guess. At first, it was because most of my free time was spent getting stuff picked out for my room at Mom's new apartment. Then, once I started shuffling back and forth between my parents, it was like my sketching time disappeared, because each of them wanted Christa time. Or I stopped wanting to sketch. Or maybe a combination of both.

The alarm on my phone beeps, and I realize it's almost time to do the next dare. The group is heading back out to the piazza anyway, and I grab Madison's sleeve. "Do you think we could climb to the top of the bell tower?" I ask first because I really don't want to get into any more trouble by going off on my own. Especially now.

"Sure," she says. "Let's see who else wants to come." Colby is in, of course. Logan, Kylie, and Owen decide to stay in the piazza with Miles, and Sasha seems to be debating whether to join us or them.

"Come with us," I say, surprising myself. "When else are you going to get to climb exactly four hundred and fourteen steps, right? Maybe you can even sketch the view from the top."

That seems to decide it for her. The four of us make our way to the bell tower, and with aching thighs soon breathlessly arrive at the top. The view is incredible. All of the city unfolds before us, red rooftops crouching over brilliantly lit windows, block after block of beautiful old buildings stretching out on every side until they reach the shadowy humps of the low-lying hills in the distance. From here we can see the big dome of the cathedral and down into the piazza with its Christmas tree that rules all Christmas trees and the little LED fairy lights that are shooting up against the dusky skyline of Florence. The spires and points are silhouetted against an orange-and-purple-streaked sunset.

"Wow," I say.

"Seriously wow." Sasha flips open her sketch pad, moving away from me toward an exterior light so she can see. Colby is pointing out something to Madison, so I'm all alone when Dad's text comes in.

Nothing can change the wonder of Christmas. He sends me a picture of him standing out in the snow. I recognize the location immediately, because we've gone there nearly every year. It's our neighborhood tree lighting, but this year he's there all alone.

I don't reply, because I'm not sure if Dad is really right or not. Our family has changed. And Christmas isn't the same this year. Not at all. Maybe if he knew that some other guy is trying to take his place, he would understand that. I shove my phone back in my pocket, but when I look back at the magnificent skyline, everything seems a little duller.

Madison comes over to tell me it's almost time to go. "Some view, huh?" she says afterward, and I nod. I snap a pic to send Dani, and try to put aside the problem of my changing family.

After rejoining the others, we return to the hotel, where Madison reminds us all of the girls' slumber-party plans.

"Ooooh, so fun!" Kylie squeals, but I hesitate. I'm only even considering going because I need an excuse to avoid Mom. That, and because I liked talking about art with Sasha. But right then, another text from Dad comes through, asking if I got his text or not, and all the sad feelings of our changing family come rushing back in.

"I think I'll pass tonight, Madison," I say. "I'm wiped. And I need to text my dad."

"That's fine," she says with a smile. "Know your limits. We'll do another slumber party the last night in Paris and you can join in then. Well, Sasha and Kylie? Let's do this. Candy, nail polish, and movies are waiting for us."

Sasha looks a bit bummed as they head off to the elevators. Part of me wishes I could explain, but retreating to my room is so much easier. I'm relieved to discover that Mom is still out. I send a quick text to my dad saying that Florence has been wonderful and the lights are cool and I'm happy for the dares, dodging everything I'm really feeling. And then I spend the rest of the night swiping through the recent photos Dani's posted online, which leads me to pics my other Chicago friends have taken, and I scroll through their histories, going all the way back to last December, when we were together having our usual Christmastime fun. It all seems like a different life, and I realize everything I'm seeing reminds me how *much* things have changed since this time last year. Dad is wrong. Something has changed the wonder of Christmas for our family. And there's absolutely nothing I can do about it.

13

I SPEND THE MORNING PACKING, because today we fly from Florence to Paris for the next leg of the tour. My friendly bellman never knocks on my door, so at lunchtime I text Dad to see what's up.

Next dare won't come until Thursday. Know you will need all your energy for mom-daughter fun.

I groan both at the cheesiness of the text and the thought of all the awkwardness with mom-daughter fun ahead of me. Thursday is two days away. Sure, it would be hard to complete any dares while not telling Mom about them, but at least it would have been a distraction.

Things have gotten weirder between us. It's like Mom knows that I'm upset about something so she's being extra chatty. But *she's* also upset with *me* about not telling her what I'm upset about *and* the fact that I never came to any of the theater performances in Italy, so she keeps giving me *the look* that means she's not 100 percent thrilled with me right now. I spend most of the flight from Italy to France avoiding her by wandering around the plane to where the other kids are sitting, and then I invite Colby to come back to our row, where there's an empty seat. Colby tells Mom about all his favorite spots in Paris. Mom seems to like Colby, and it's way less awkward with both of them around.

This helps a lot when we're actually in Paris, and I ask Colby to come along on every activity Mom has planned for me and her. We manage to avoid any heart-to-hearts because the days are crammed full of things to do. Mom and Colby joke their way around the city tour, where the landscape of Paris sprawls more magnificently than in every painting I've ever seen. We sightsee during the day, but nighttime in the city is my favorite, because Paris knows how to decorate for Christmas. Lit evergreen archways line all the main thoroughfares, and there are Christmas trees everywhere. In front of the Eiffel Tower. Outside the cathedrals. In the shopping centers. We see museums and frost-covered parks, cafés and boutiques. Mom takes us on a walking tour past some of the famous fashion houses, and we have fun gawking at all the crazy window displays of stuff nobody would actually ever wear. We ramble through Notre Dame, and I find once again the holy quiet that seems to pervade those old churches set in the middle of bustling, living cities.

Later that night Mom finds *Home Alone* online, and she and I watch it while consuming mounds of French pastries and candy (totally safe ones, of course). *Home Alone* is up there on my all-time favorite Christmas movies list, not because it's such a winner—there are loads of better ones, especially the old classics—but because it was the first one I saw that made me fall in love with Christmas. I was tiny, like five or six, when I watched it, and I loved how the McCallister house looked all decorated with lights everywhere and snow outside. For years I begged my parents to have another kid because, however obnoxious Kevin's family was, it was so cool how much energy and life they all had. But Mom and Dad didn't go for it, which, given how things turned out with them, is probably good. But still, a few hours watching Kevin's outrageous pranks is an annual tradition at my house. Mom and I quote over half the movie to each other. I like this version of Mom: the one who seems able to join in on the fun, and the one who hasn't once mentioned S.T. for the entire two days.

On Thursday morning, my phone chimes a reminder that the fifth dare is coming. As if I would have forgotten. At this hotel, there is no friendly deliveryman. Someone from the front desk phones up to let me know that "Mademoiselle Christa Vasile has a parcel waiting." I like how official it sounds, especially with the nasal French accent, so, after saying good-bye to Mom, I stop by on the way to the breakfast room, where I'm supposed to meet up with M&M and the rest of the kids. The front desk is busy with guests checking out, and the clerk hands me a padded envelope without much fanfare.

"Is this all?" I say, confused, but the clerk is not in the mood to chat and offers me a smile and a brusque *"Mais oui, bien sûr."* Which I know from French class means, "But yes, of course."

The gift tag tucked inside has Nutcrackers playing trumpets on it and says: #5: DARE YOU TO DISCOVER THE MUSIC OF THE NIGHT. There's also a thick stack of tickets with a Post-it note telling me to give them to Madison. Even though the tickets are all in French, I know that "The Music of the Night" is a song from *The Phantom of the Opera* and guess that the tickets have something to do with that. I'm not a big musical fan, but Dani has forced me to watch a few, and who doesn't love *Phantom*? I wonder if

Dani was somehow behind this dare. She's always trying to convince me to appreciate how music is the "soundtrack to life" and will help me get in touch with my emotions and blah blah blah. I text her with a pic of the tickets. She will lose her mind over them.

The hotel breakfasts in Paris are vastly superior to those in Florence. Pastries, croissants, and . . . thick liquid chocolate to drink. Chocolate! For breakfast! The rest of the group has already gathered at a long table with M&M, so I grab a buttery croissant and a little pot of chocolate on my way to join them.

When Madison sees what's in the envelope, she totally gives a Kylie squeal. "Ohmigosh! Your dad got them!" But she won't say any more, no matter how much I pester her.

"Got *what*?" I ask in my wheedlingest voice, but Madison refuses to reveal the surprise.

I knew that Dad had known Madison was a good tour guide, but I'm finally piecing together the fact that he must have helped plan the entire itinerary. Which would be so like my dad. And makes sense of the fact that all of the dares are compatible with the scheduled outings. *Duh*.

"Please, Maddie?" Kylie won't stop with the coaxing. It's not only Madison's name she's taken to abbreviating. Chrissie is really not my favorite, but it sure beats Logie.

"Maddie, can we *not* wear the visors?" Kylie continues. "We're absolutely not going to go anywhere besides where you tell us. Right, guys?"

We all agree, and Logan holds up his hands. "Scout's honor."

Madison deliberates, but she's so happy over the Super Surprise Secret Tickets that she shrugs. "All right. Let's try it. But stay together."

Everyone cheers, and it seems like our Paris adventure is off to a good start.

Logan falls in beside me. "How was your time off?"

"Pretty good." I fill him in on all the stuff I saw. "What about you?"

"Paris is so cool." Logan rubs his hands through his spiky hair. "And then my mom and I took a trip out to the countryside. It was amazing." He tells me about the little town they explored. "It totally looked like something out of a fairy tale."

It's a bit of a walk from the hotel to the opera house, and during that time Logan and I discover that we have a lot in common: we both have the same top Christmas movie of all time—hello, *The Muppet Christmas Carol*—we both could eat chocolate and mint candies all day long but *never* chocolate and peanut butter, and neither of us has ever been to Disney World. And then there are the things not-so-in-common: he loves spicy food, can hardly sit still, and spends all his time not-parkouring reading some comic book series I've never heard of. But by the end of the walk, I feel like I'm getting to know Logan a little better, and he seems pretty cool.

When we arrive at the Palais Garnier, which is Paris's most famous opera house, we circle up around Madison. Behind her, the impressive building looms in all its over-the-top glory. It's huge. We've seen so much old European architecture by this point that the buildings kind of look the same, but this one dwarfs them all with its evenly spaced archways and the golden statues marking the exterior. Madison gives her usual "be culturally sensitive" spiel, and then we're headed inside. Logan swings over some wrought-iron handrails on the stairs we have to climb, which of course earns him a frown from Madison and an admiring clap from Kylie.

Colby appears at my shoulder as we follow them up. He feels like an old friend after all we've been through. "No handrail leaps for you?" I ask him with a smile.

"Naw," he says with a grin. "Definitely not on Madison's Good Behavior for Americans in France list."

I laugh as ahead of us Kylie urges Logan to do one

more round and, after a careful glance at Madison, who is conferring with Miles, he obliges.

"I think Logan is into Kylie," Colby confides in me. "He just can't work up the courage to tell her."

"Into Kylie?" I say, catching myself in time to keep the surprise out of my voice. Admittedly Kylie's grown on me, despite the nicknames. Her main fault now is being connected with S.T., and I doubt Logan cares about that.

"Yeah," Colby says. "Poor guy."

"Aw," I say, coming to Kylie's defense, "she's not so bad."

"I didn't mean that! Not at all!" Colby waves his hands defensively. "Kylie's great. Really. I just mean poor guy in that he's so into a girl and she doesn't think of him as more than a friend." For some reason his cheeks have turned really red and he's shoved his hands deep into his pockets.

"Oh," I say as an uncomfortable thought presents itself. Is Colby into Kylie, too? I feel embarrassed. Embarrassed that I thought Colby and I were such good friends and he never mentioned Kylie to me. And embarrassed because he is so embarrassed. Fortunately, at that moment, Owen joins us, and he—being oblivious to all embarrassment—interrupts our conversation by telling us how similar the architecture of the opera house is to the description of Gringotts Bank in the Harry Potter series.

"Epic," Owen says when we walk into the foyer with its ginormous chandeliers and gaudily painted ceiling. "Definitely not made by Muggles."

I giggle, overly relieved that whatever the moment with Colby was has passed, and shove Owen playfully on the shoulder. "Are you *sure* you're a Muggle? Or are you secretly about to head off to wizarding school?"

"I wish," he says. "I'd do anything to be in Gryffindor House."

We talk Harry Potter houses while we wait for the tour to start. Colby settles on Ravenclaw, and I choose Hufflepuff.

"I always feel a little sorry for the Hufflepuffs," I explain. "They never have anything exciting happen to them."

Owen looks at me with newfound appreciation. "I could get on board with Hufflepuff."

"We can't all be Hufflepuff," Colby says, a little heatedly. "Besides. There have to be four houses." Colby actually sounds worked up about this. The others join us then, and when she hears what we're talking about, Kylie says, "I'd definitely be Slytherin. Their colors are the best."

"I'd be Slytherin, too," Logan says, almost too quickly.

Owen makes a scornful sound. "You can't pick a house

based on colors, Kylie."

"Why not?" Colby says. "Who says she can't be Slytherin?" I give Colby a funny look. Since when does he care so much about Harry Potter stuff? But then I see that he's almost glaring at Owen. Maybe this isn't about Harry Potter stuff. Maybe it's about a girl. Maybe it's about Kylie. The uncomfortable feeling is back, but I don't know why.

"What about you, Sasha?" I say, so I don't have to think about what that feeling might mean.

"Meh." She shrugs. "Any of them, I guess. I'm not a big fan."

Owen looks at me. "Did she really say what I think she said?"

Colby is glaring at Owen again, and I don't think I can take any more of the uncomfortableness.

"Okay, okay," I say. "The Sorting Hat will pick Sasha's house. Isn't that how it should work anyway?"

"Good point, Christa," Owen says admiringly, and then turns to Sasha. "Maybe you just haven't read them enough times. . . ."

Just then our tour starts, and M&M herd us forward past the ginormous red Christmas tree in the lobby (well done, Paris!), and Colby falls into step beside me.

He's kind of glaring at Owen, and I wonder if he's still

upset about what Owen said to Kylie.

"Are you okay?" I ask, but I don't really want to know the answer. What if he tells me how much *he* likes Kylie, too? The one thing worse than all of Kylie's boy-craziness would be to have to hear how all the boys are crazy for her.

"Not important," he mumbles. "Not everyone likes Harry Potter, I guess."

Our tour guide leads us into a small dark room with padded seats. I choose one between Sasha and Kylie to avoid the weird vibe I'm getting from Colby. We watch a short documentary that explains that *The Phantom of the Opera* is based on events that supposedly took place in this opera house. Soon, I forget all about the Harry Potter House Controversy and Colby's weirdness, because I'm sucked into the weirdness that is the plot to *Phantom of the Opera*, which, basically, is how a super-creepy guy who lives under an opera house pines for an actress he can't get. I know it's famous and everything, but hello! Stalker much? Even though I know the phantom is so not a hero, when I hear the eerie notes of "The Music of the Night," I feel a bit unsteady inside, like I might cry, which makes no sense at all. *Shut up, Dani,* I mentally tell her voice, which is reminding me to let my feelings flow.

"That is *so* beautiful." Kylie is crying when it ends.

"What a tragic story."

Sasha is quiet, her head bent over her sketchbook, and even Logan is still and mellow.

"Yeah. Really beautiful," Logan says, glancing over at us girls.

Madison pulls out the tickets, which the guide reveals to be special behind-the-scenes passes for a tour to the tunnels underneath the opera house, where the Phantom supposedly lived.

We walk down an old stairwell that takes us into the damp underground spaces of a really old city. I'm not going to lie. However cool it is to be all behind the scenes and everything, it supremely stinks down here. Like gross, hold-your-sleeve-over-your-nose stinkage.

Kylie pinches her nose in her fingers dramatically, and the boys keep making fart jokes. Even chill Sasha has her collar up to block the smell.

The walls are moist, and we can hear drips on old stone. If the Phantom really did live down here in one of the tunnels the guide keeps pointing out to us, I feel super sorry for him.

Finally, we reach an underground lake. The surface is smooth as glass, pooling around weathered stone columns. Far off, an opening overhead lets in a cloud of light that shines down on the murky depths. It's beautiful in an eerie sort of way. There are benches near the edge, and we sit while the guide tells us how the lake was part of the setting for the original *Phantom* novel.

I look at the mysterious water. Why did Dad want me to come here? There were no happy endings for the Phantom—in real life, or in the musical.

I fold my tour brochure into a little paper boat like the kind I used to set sail in the turbulent waters of Buckingham Fountain back in Chicago. The guide plays us a compilation of the songs, and the haunting music fills the chamber. She explains how the classic themes of love and rejection stir universal human emotions in us and that is why the musical endures even after all these years. I listen to the melody, and it makes me feel quiet and still inside. I think about the dares and how Dad has planned them for me to have all the way over here in Europe. I'm glad for that—at least *something* is feeling the way Christmas is supposed to—but I'm also kind of sad about them. I mean, usually I do the scavenger hunt in one crazy night, and afterward Dad and I stay up late and look at pictures from all the stages of the hunt. And Dad isn't here. I miss him. And home.

The melody swells, and I realize my homesickness

grows along with it. I don't exactly feel like I'm going to cry or anything, but I do wish I could go right back to the hotel and crawl under the covers and hide for an hour or two. The music begins to fade as the song ends, and I shift my feet to bring myself back to the present. Whew! Dani is right. Music does unleash all the feels. It's not so much that the music made me sad, but it showed me the part of me deep inside that already was sad. *The Phantom of the Opera* is a sad story, and so is the music. But maybe love stories always have tragic endings. Maybe all you're left with is feeling sad and afraid when the happy ending doesn't come. Before I turn to follow the others back up and outside, I set my little boat to sail on the lake and leave it there alone in the dark.

14

THE NEXT MORNING A BAG wrapped in muted tissue paper is waiting for me at the front desk. Inside, I find an art kit full of watercolors, pastels, sketch pencils, and paper. They all have that new-wood smell fresh from the store. I'm sitting at a corner table in the lobby exploring them over a pot of morning chocolate when I hear someone come up next to me.

"Wow," Sasha says. "That's an impressive stash."

"Totally," I say. "My dad sent them to me. Here." I shove aside the tissue paper. "Sit down and check them out with me."

"This is the best brand of pencil to sketch with," Sasha says, turning each over in her hands very carefully.

When M&M come over to tell us it's time to leave the hotel, I'm surprised that a whole hour has gone by. When I get up from the table I see that there's more in the bottom of the bag—a bright red scarf, a hat, fingerless gloves, and the note I ignored earlier in my exploration of all the new supplies. The gift tag has a Christmas wreath on it and reads: #6: DARE YOU TO BE INSPIRED AT THE LOUVRE. I'm not too surprised to discover that the famous museum is our destination today, since I now get that Dad has carefully coordinated all the dares with our tour itinerary.

As Sasha and I walk with the others, she tells me how the Louvre has been her favorite place thus far. "I wish we had more than a day there," she says wistfully. "I've already been there twice on our off days, and there's so much more I still want to see."

We cross a bridge that is covered with the same padlocks I saw in Florence. What is with people and their crazy love locks? As we move farther along, most of the locks are blocked by the artists who are crowded near the edges.

"Want a picture done?" a man offers.

"A caricature!" someone else cries out.

All of them have little portable easels set up where they are happily working away, selling paintings of famous landscapes to tourists or doing quick, funny sketches of the people themselves.

I walk by some watercolors that show whimsical scenes

from nature: a fairy house in the woods, elfin children gathering shells by the water, and little animals tending their shared cottage.

"These are so fun," I say as Sasha and I flip through them.

"How long have you been painting?" Sasha surprises me by talking to the artist, who looks like she might be a college student.

The artist explains that she's studying at the Paris College of Art and comes here in her free hours to sell her work.

"And you?" she asks in her charming French accent. "Are you artists?"

Sasha and I exchange shy glances, but the girl has already spied my traveling case.

"But of course! You even have your kit with you." She points to an empty spot next to her. "Join me! Paint!"

I look wistfully at the spot, but M&M are already waiting for us up ahead.

"I don't think I can, though thanks for the offer," I say.

"Wait." Sasha pulls out a crumpled itinerary. "It says we have our lunch break to explore the Louvre gardens. Let's ask if we can come back here and paint instead." She turns to our new friend. "Will you be here all day?"

"*Bien sûr*," she replies.

"Then we might be back. We'll try." Sasha squeezes my arm as we hurry to catch up to the others. "This is so cool! I can't believe it!"

I'm having trouble believing it myself. I feel a flicker of my old enthusiasm for art return. It's been a long time since I've spent a few hours wandering around Oak Park sketching my favorite corners of the neighborhood. Dad hasn't given me specific instructions for what it means to be "inspired" at the Louvre, so I suppose Sasha's idea is a good way to complete it.

"So can we?" Sasha asks M&M as we enter the enormous square that flanks the famous pyramid-like entrance to the Louvre. "You'll know exactly where we are the whole time and everything."

Madison looks uncertain, but Miles jumps in. "It's cool. I can hang with them, so whoever wants to be artsy can do their thing, and you can take whoever wants to go to the gardens there to do their thing."

"Ohmigosh, Miles. You are the best." Kylie hasn't resorted to calling him Mylie yet, but she's come close. From the corner of my eye, I can see Colby watching us, and I think about how pretty Kylie looks today. But really? Does Colby really like Kylie? Like *like* Kylie?

Kylie launches into a diatribe about how much she loves art. "I do tons of projects on Pinterest and stuff," she says.

I sigh. Kylie has grown on me, but seriously! Someone needs to tell the girl that Pinterest does *not* equal art. I am not that person, so instead I stay quiet and move quickly out of earshot when we enter the museum.

Sasha and I spend the morning hovering on the fringes of our group as we make our way through the second floor of the Louvre, which houses paintings, prints, and drawings. Sasha is the perfect museum companion—quiet, reflective, and not annoying.

Kylie seems to have latched on to Colby in my absence, tugging him around the galleries.

"Ohmigosh, Colby. You *have* to see this." Occasionally he shoots me a smile or a bemused glance. Once, when Kylie's distracted by a drinking fountain, he tells me that Logan has asked him to try to figure out if Kylie likes him or not. I nod but wonder if he's just too embarrassed to admit the truth.

The morning hours fly by, and before we know it, Miles is delivering our sack lunches and rounding up everyone who wants to go to the artists' bridge. It's chilly out, with the clouded skies foreboding rain, so I put on my new hat, scarf, and gloves. I like that the bright red fabric makes me feel just a bit more artsy, and I might need every bit of that if I'm supposed to get inspired again.

"Ah, you've returned," says our artist friend, who we learn is named Nicole. She graciously makes extra room for both me and Sasha next to her, and soon our mini station is set up. Sasha has brought her own sketch pad and pencils, but I tell her she should feel free to use any of my supplies as well.

"I think I'm going to try out the charcoals," I say. "Make a Christmas scene of the Champs-Élysées." We drive by it on almost every outing, and I'm pretty sure I can reconstruct a cool interpretation from memory.

Soon, everything in me is focused on the grays and blacks of the scene slowly emerging on my paper. I hear the sound of people passing by, of customers visiting Nicole's station, of rustling papers tossed about in the winter air. But it's all background noise. I've completed three views of the famous landmark when Miles finally interrupts.

"We have to return to the hotel in an hour. I don't know if you want to see more inside or stay out here." I look up to discover that we've sketched the whole afternoon away. Nicole is packing up her things, and the gloomy winter sky is darkening as the afternoon leans toward dusk.

"You seemed really into it," Miles explains when I ask

him what happened to the lunch hour. "I didn't want to break your concentration."

I pack up my half-eaten, forgotten sandwich and other supplies. Sasha looks the most relaxed and happy I've seen her, and I wonder if my face has the same mellow peacefulness.

"That was fantastic!" I prop my drawings up on the bench behind me so I can put away my supplies. It really was. Inside I feel like old, forgotten pieces of me have been aired out and given space to breathe again. As if to underscore the moment, it begins to snow, sending delicate white flakes onto my coat and gloves.

"How perfect is this?" I ask Sasha, pointing at the sky.

"Coldly perfect?" she says, wrinkling up her nose. "I'm not a fan."

What? Snow means winter. Snow means *Christmas*! But I keep my thoughts to myself and finish packing up.

Miles is exchanging phone numbers with Nicole, and I wonder if that's the real reason he offered to chaperone us and stay longer.

Just then, a girl approaches me and rattles off something my first-year French can't interpret. Nicole translates for us.

"She's interested in one of your sketches," Nicole says, pointing at the three I've leaned against the bench. "For a

Christmas present for her mother."

"Um," I say, wondering if I should tell the girl that I'm not a real artist. Or that they're not for sale. Or that she's making a big mistake.

"Ten euros," Nicole says when she sees I don't know how to answer. My eyes about pop out of my head, but I don't contradict her, especially when the girl slips her a bill without blinking an eye.

Nicole hands me the money with a wink before wrapping up the drawing in some of her special tissue paper before placing it in a silver holiday bag.

"*Merci*," I say to the girl. "Merry Christmas."

After she leaves, Sasha grabs my arm and lets out the closest thing to a squeal I've ever heard from her. "She wanted your work! That is so cool!"

"I know!" I might be squealing as well. "Wow!"

Creating art again feels *right*, and a piece of me I've missed seems to fall back into place.

Later, when I'm back in my suite, I carefully wrap my other two sketches in tissue to pack them in a zippered pocket of my suitcase. I'll give one to Dad, and I'll keep one for myself to remember the moment. Who knows? Maybe one day I'll come back and go to the Paris College of Art like Nicole.

Mom comes in after her performance and flops down

on the suite couch. "How was your day? Oh!" She points to my little pile of art supplies. "Did you sketch something?" She pops up, energized, and peeks under the tissue paper at one of my creations. "Hon, that's gorgeous. I love the smudged blacks and grays and then the one dot of bright red in the umbrella. So Paris."

For once on this trip I think I might like connecting with Mom. Maybe it's the good feeling overflowing from the afternoon, or maybe it's just that things might be getting better between us. I decide to tell her about selling my first picture.

"It was so nice to sketch again. Like coming home or something." I laugh when I say this last part, because I know it sounds sort of cheesy, but Mom takes me seriously.

"The creative part of you *is* a piece of your home," she says. "I know exactly what you mean. My old theater director used to say that when you discover the instinct to create, you discover yourself. I think there's a little piece of me in each character I play. Do you feel that way about what you create?"

I think about this. "Maybe. I mean, I don't always draw people, but whatever I'm working on is a piece of what I'm feeling, you know?"

Mom tucks her feet up under her. "Exactly. It helps us

access pieces of ourselves we maybe didn't even know were there."

"Totally." I think about the way the music at the *Phantom of the Opera* exhibit also did exactly that. "I think my art helps make me more of who I am."

For one tiny moment it's as though we're not the mother and daughter who have been awkwardly enduring the past few days. We're artists talking about our *craft*. Kind of like they do in the behind-the-scenes clips of DVDs. But then there's a knock on the door. And it's S.T. standing there asking if he can speak with Mom in the lobby. And Mom goes.

When the door shuts behind her, I put the artwork away. Somehow it seems a little less magical. I change into my pj's and get ready for bed. It's really late when the suite door opens and I hear Mom creep in. When she's in the bathroom, I peek at my cell. One a.m. I wonder what S.T. needed to say that was so important it couldn't wait until morning. Well, until later in the morning. I don't feel like a creative working on her craft anymore. I'm back to being just a girl who can't figure out what's going on with her parents. And I have a mom who doesn't seem to be able to either.

15

TODAY THE FRONT DESK CLERK hands me a long flat box covered in reindeer wrapping paper. I follow my usual Paris morning ritual of piling my plate high with croissants, grabbing a pot of chocolate, and claiming a corner table in the breakfast room. While I'm waiting for my drink to cool, I open the box. Inside is a chef's hat and apron in fabric that's dotted all over with little Christmas cookies. The attached gift tag with gingerbread people on it reads: **#7: DARE YOU TO TRY SOMETHING NEW.** The additional instructions tell me to go to Fouquet's on the Champs-Élysées at eight p.m.

The guidebook tells me that Fouquet's is a famous French restaurant that's been around for over a hundred years. It gives it five stars and five dollar signs, which means it's really fancy. With a feeling of misgiving, I tuck the dare note into the book to mark the page. Fancy food is so not my thing. And, obviously, neither is trying anything new, especially when it's paired with a restaurant. Basically, fancy French food in an expensive restaurant sounds like a nightmare.

"What's that?" Mom's voice surprises me as she points to the package and plops down at my table. Most mornings she's still in the suite when I leave, but today, she's already dressed, makeup on, and apparently is joining me for breakfast.

"Just something Dad sent," I mumble. "You know. For the Christmas scavenger hunt." I don't know why, but I really, really, really don't want to talk to Mom about the dares. I know we had our bonding moment and everything last night, but the dares feel special and connected my old life, and a part of me is afraid that talking about them will ruin that. Besides, if I tell Mom all the details, she might tell S.T. or something.

"Gotcha." She folds her hands in front of her, tapping her red-painted fingernails slowly on the shiny tabletop. "So. Last day in Paris. Big plans?"

I pull out the crumpled itinerary from my bag. "I think we're supposed to visit the Musée d'Orsay," I say, and then quickly add, "And then the Champs-Élysées later tonight." I'm not sure how I'll get there exactly, but maybe M&M will have a suggestion.

"Well, if you have some free time in the itinerary, I'd love it if you could squeeze in coming to our performance," Mom says in a carefully neutral tone. "Maybe after the Champs-Élysées?"

"Oooh," I say in a totally fake disappointed tone. I show her the itinerary and the thing I had forgotten to include: Madison's promised slumber party. "I promised the girls I'd be at this one—it's my last chance to do it, I guess." Mom is chewing her lip like she does when she's less than thrilled about things. "There's extra performances in London for Christmas week, right? I'm sure I'll have some free time then. I'll catch it in London. I promise."

"Okay," Mom says, and takes a slow slurp of her coffee. I doubt I'm fooling her. It's not that I don't want to see her show, it's that . . . well . . . I guess it *is* that I don't want to see it. There's the whole feeling weird about not being at her performance with Dad thing, but I think there's something else, too. I mean, I know being an actor is a huge part of who she is, but she also started going to more and more auditions right around the time things started getting weird at home. It's hard not to think that maybe

Mom's new career goals might have something to do with the divorce.

I wish I could figure out how to tell her some of what I'm feeling. Or, even better, that I didn't have to tell her it at all, that she could get it without me having to try to say it, but I think if I try, Mom won't understand. I mean, her only daughter keeps ditching her play. It makes sense that she's upset about it, but I still can't make myself go to her play. I don't say anything at all.

Mom trickles a little stream from my chocolate pot into her travel coffee mug and then gathers up the rest of her things. "I hope you have a good day, Christa."

"You, too, Mom," I say in a miserable voice. I'm relieved when she leaves, but I know that not having to talk about what's wrong won't make it go away.

Later that night when we get back from our full day of touring, a bellman taps my shoulder before we even make it through the lobby. "Mademoiselle Vasile?" he asks in a perfect French accent. "I have a message for you. From your father." He gives Colby, who is hanging back with me, a skeptical look. "But only for Mademoiselle Vasile."

Colby has been more normal today. I don't know if it's because he's given up on Kylie, who has been totally hanging out with Logan, or if he's over whatever it was that was making him weird the other day, but I'm just glad to have my friend back.

"He can come with me," I say, because I know this probably has to do with tonight's restaurant dare, and I could use some moral support. The bellman nods and ushers us past the breakfast room to a small private-looking library. Closing the double doors, he points to a leather sofa.

"Have a seat."

With crisp efficiency, the man produces a tablet that he taps on for a few moments until the crooning voice of Nat King Cole drifts toward me. I clap my hands. This is the song we've always decorated the tree to back at home! The hotel man sets the tablet on a little stand and puts a pitcher and cup next to it before bowing. "I will be out in the hallway if you need anything."

"*Merci*," I say, fumbling for a tip, but the bellman looks offended.

"Your father has taken care of everything," he says stiffly, and then disappears.

A few seconds later, Dad's voice comes from the screen, and I see him peering into the tablet. "Hey, sweetie. Have some eggnog." I peek into the fancy hotel pitcher and see that somehow Dad has found a way to get one of my favorite Christmastime treats delivered.

"Aw, Colby, look!" I pour some into a glass. "Hey, you should ask the hotel guy for another glass."

"It's okay," Colby says.

"So this is the Colby I've heard so much about," Dad says.

"It's a pleasure to meet you, Mr. Vasile."

I shoot Colby a look. He sounds as formal as the hotel man!

"Thank you for being such a great tour guide for Christa," Dad says. "Her mom has told me how much fun you all have had together."

Wait. *Mom* has been talking to *Dad*? I wonder if she's told him everything about *her* trip, too. I sip the eggnog while we talk about how great the dares have been. After a while, Colby excuses himself. "I should go. It was nice to talking with you."

Before Colby's even out of the room, Dad starts teasing me. "So, Colby, hmm? Is he a thing? Like a boyfriend kind of thing?"

"*DAD*," I say, shooting Colby an apologetic look. "Colby's just a friend." The only thing that could make Colby being all awkward about liking Kylie *more* awkward is if he thinks I like him or something, too. Colby waves and shuts the door behind him, but he has a funny look on his face.

Ugh. I wish he hadn't heard that. Horrible timing.

Dad doesn't seem to notice and instead tells me that he's tweaking this latest dare just a little bit. "I've found a way for you to bring a friend or two with you tonight. I've cleared it all with Madison, who will take you there and back. She says you girls have a slumber party planned for later, so I thought you might want to invite Kylie and Sasha." He pauses with a smirk. "But maybe you'd rather have the night out with Colby?"

Of course it would be fun to do tonight's dare with Colby, but there is no way I can tell that to Dad now or he'll never stop teasing me. And, worse, it will be weird to see Colby right after he overheard Dad. It would be almost like a date. With Madison as a chaperone. And when Colby really wishes he could be out with Kylie. *So awful.*

"I'll ask Sasha to come with me," I say. "I've been getting to know her better lately. We both like art." I tell him about the Louvre and the Paris College of Art and maybe coming back to study when I'm older. Dad tells me about how Chicago got a big snowstorm that almost canceled the big neighborhood Christmas party.

"Everyone asked about you," he says. "Mrs. Wilson even made the peppermint fudge you like."

"Save me some?" I feel a wave of homesickness when

I think of how last year all three of us went and chowed down on Mrs. Wilson's baking. Before I know it, Dad says it's probably time to say good-bye so I can go meet up with Madison, and I realize he's right. We've been talking for almost an hour.

"I'm glad you're making friends, Chris," he says before telling me good-bye. And as I leave the little library, I realize he's right. I like the other kids. We're having fun together. We *are* friends.

My new friends are all hanging out in a corner of the hotel lobby. Shockingly, Owen is not reading Harry Potter for once. Instead, he's flipping through one of Logan's graphic novels. Logan slouches on the couch with his eyes closed and earbuds in. Colby is chatting with Kylie, who is sitting by the fireplace sipping something from a mug. I get that funny squirmy feeling inside when I see them together, and then I shove it aside. Why should I care if Colby likes Kylie? He can be friends with more than just me. I spot Sasha over in the corner scrolling through her phone, and I make my way toward her.

"Hey," I say as she looks up. "Do you have plans for later tonight?"

She shrugs but then seems interested when I tell her about the restaurant. "It has something to do with cooking,"

I say, "but I'm not exactly sure what."

"Cooking?" Kylie squeals from behind me. "Ohmigosh, French cooking! Can I come, Chrissie? Please? Pretty, pretty please?"

I think about saying I can only bring one person and that maybe she should stay and get some time with Colby, but only for half a second.

"Totally," I say. "It will be like phase one of girls' night."

"Ohmigosh!" Kylie claps her hands and bounces up and down on her toes, which is kind of how I feel on the inside. Minus the excited part. And amp up the nervous jitters. I can't believe I'm going to a cooking thing. In France. I don't even have Benadryl on me in case I have an allergic reaction!

Soon, Madison has us all bundled up and into the cab that will take us to the restaurant. It's situated on a corner, and the whole exterior glows red with holiday lights around the cursive neon sign reading "Fouquet's." We walk up the carpeted entrance, which is flanked by a row of perfectly manicured Christmas trees wrapped with even swirls of white lights. Once inside, Madison turns us over to a Frenchwoman who weaves her way through the crowded dining area, set with crisply draped tablecloths and fine china, to a back kitchen that seems designed for private lessons or filming cooking shows or something.

The woman gives us all chef's jackets—no tiny Christmas trees on these, just a thick white fabric that buttons up the back—and invites us to gather around a shiny stainless-steel table.

"*Bien*," she says. "*Je m'appelle* Dominique, and I love to cook. Now you tell me why you are here and your favorite kind of food."

Awesome. Is it possible to tell her that I'm here because I *have* to be, because there's no way I'm going to forfeit on the dares over a *food* challenge, and that my favorite kinds of foods are the ones I know are safe, which I realize are not the ones we're about to be touching and smelling and eating? Nervous inner me feels like she's moved on from bouncing around on tiptoes to wanting to barf.

Kylie has no hesitation. She introduces herself with a cheery smile. "I love food. Reading about it. Watching it on TV. Eating it." She giggles. "Ohmigosh, I can't believe I'm going to learn how to cook French food in *Paris!*"

Sasha explains how she feels food can be a form of artistic expression. "I like baking. Icing cakes. Decorating desserts. That sort of thing."

"My turn?" I say when I realize it's gone all quiet. Madison isn't participating. She's sitting off to one side of the room, fixated on her phone.

"Um, my dad likes to kind of surprise me?" I say lamely. "And this was his surprise?" I'm not sure why I'm saying those things like they're questions, but nervous inner me is about to lose her head, because I've just spotted shrimp and crab over on a side table under the window. Shellfish is like the number-one allergy that can show up without warning. And then there's also the fact that shrimps are basically the cockroaches of the sea. Gross.

"*Bon*," Dominique says. "And what is your favorite food?"

My palms feel sweaty and I take a few steps to the side, farther away from the shellfish extravaganza going on over there. "Pizza," I say, almost apologetically. "I kind of like basic things. Oh! And chocolate!"

"Aaaah." Dominique grins. "Chocolate. A gem among foods. You must be a true connoisseur, *non*? Now. Let's get started with the appetizer course."

I brace myself for the shellfish onslaught and wonder what happens if you suddenly get allergic to something you don't know you're allergic to and then you smell it. Or touch it. Wait, can you have a reaction if you just *touch* a food? But miracle of miracles, Dominique does not move to the shellfish pile. Instead, she pulls a wedge of flat, creamy cheese out of the fridge. It's not safe mozzarella, but it's a thousand times better than shellfish.

Dominique sets out little cheese knives. "All good chefs must taste their ingredients. This is Camembert. Take a taste and describe it for me."

I grip the little knife in my sweaty hands and wonder whether if I stab myself with it I can be excused from the class and go back to the hotel. Should I go ahead and fess up that the thought of cinnamon blended into my chocolate stresses me out, so there's absolutely no *way* I'm going to eat something I can't pronounce that smells really gross? Besides, don't all fancy cheeses have mold in them or something? No way am I eating mold.

Kylie dives right in. "Ohmigosh, that's heavenly!" she says, reaching for another slice of baguette to spread it on.

Sasha is less enthusiastic but still takes some, and as I watch them I wonder what it would be like to jump right in and enjoy the unknown again. What would it be like to eat the way I used to eat, to not think twice and just put a bite into my mouth? To be excited about trying something like I used to be about ordering the Pizza Surprise for takeout instead of calculating reactions and symptoms and what-do-I-do-if? I can't make myself not think twice, but I do manage a tiny taste on the edge of the bread, which, if you haven't tried any new foods in almost two months, is a big achievement.

It gets a little easier after that. Dominique shows us how to make traditional French crepes, which are basically a fancier and more delicate form of pancakes, and pancakes are definitely on my safe list of foods, so *phew!* Getting them thin enough is super challenging, and then there's this whole trick of not letting them tear when you have to flip them in the pan. But by the end, I've made a beautiful crepe stuffed with berries and topped with whipped cream (oh, yes!) and a tiny sprig of mint. And, for once, I am one of those people who decide to post their food online.

"I'm jelly!" Kylie says as I take the shot. "Yours looks way better than mine. You're a natural, Christa." At least Kylie has dropped her annoying cutesy nickname for me.

By the time we make the salad I realize I'm actually having fun. At a restaurant. Eating new foods. (Gasp!) Well, sort of eating them. Taking tiny tastes of new foods.

With Dominique's prompting, Kylie tells us about her earliest food memory, which is picking apples from her grandmother's orchard. Sasha's is dipping a fresh-baked cookie in milk. And mine? Well, that's easy. Mine is watching Mom and Dad make a gingerbread house together and helping to put the little candies into the white icing. Dominique keeps tossing out food-related questions that provoke some interesting answers.

I learn that Kylie really *is* a foodie. Her grandmother is a restaurant critic and retired chef, and Kylie has been cooking with her since she was five years old. Sasha's family subsists mostly on takeout, but in the fall and winter she bakes a ton with her mom, who even has a little stand at a farmer's market.

"Well," I say when it's my turn. "I used to cook a lot with my mom and dad." I remember being a little kid and standing between them tearing lettuce for salads and punching down bread dough. "But I guess as I got older, everyone got busy. Mom had more and more evening rehearsals and performances, but we still made brunch every weekend." I don't add the part about how a year or two ago that just became a fancy cereal bar. I don't tell them that the fun times in the kitchen stopped about the same time the cold silences appeared between Mom and Dad. The forced meals where Mom would suddenly clear her place and "be done," and Dad would sit sulkily staring out the window. Or the breakfasts interrupted by private, intense conversations between them out on the balcony. Or the dinners that Dad texted he would be late for, and Mom would just put the food back in the fridge with a sigh and hand me the pizza delivery menu. I don't tell them about these things, because they make me feel tight inside, and I don't even think I could choke it all out if I wanted to.

"Food is a language for our emotions," Dominique says. Her French accent makes everything she says sound wise. "How we feel about food can teach us how we feel about life."

I let that sink in for a moment. If I follow Dominique's logic, the fact that I worry about being allergic to new things that come my way means that I'm afraid of life. Which is ridiculous. I love life. And new things . . . well, new things aren't *that* bad, right? I get an uncomfortable sensation as I wonder if Dominique might be right, and if deep inside I'm on the alert against any and all changes. And if I look deeper inside, I wonder if that's because *so* much has changed that I haven't wanted to. *Whoa. Deep.* I push it all out of my mind to think about later.

Dominique is still talking about how wonderful food and our feelings are. "And nothing can make us feel more in love with life than the foods we share at a holiday feast. Here in France we have a traditional Three Kings Cake." She explains how the cake is connected to the kings who came to bring presents to Baby Jesus when he was born. And so now people hide a little plastic baby inside and whoever gets that sort of wins or something. But sometimes it's not a baby but a bean. Which is supposed to be great to get in your slice of cake. I guess I really don't get the whole thing. But who am I to judge? It's not like we don't have weird traditions. Hello, fairy who wants your old teeth so bad she sneaks in your room at night to get them.

The cake she pulls out is gorgeous and, I am happy to discover, absolutely nut-free. "You girls have earned it. Please, be my guest."

"Wait," Kylie breathes in a reverent voice. "We have to take a selfie." We all crowd in around the cake with Dominique and Madison behind us. I take one with my phone also and study it while I eat the delicious dessert. I'm not sure if I agree with everything Dominique said about food or not, but in the picture I look pretty happy. Relaxed, even.

Later, back at the hotel, I don't hesitate to join in on the slumber party. Even if it wasn't the last one, even if I hadn't told my mom I had to go to get out of seeing her play, I find that I actually want to be there, surrounded by heaps of chocolate bars, old copies of *Seventeen* magazine, and the cartoon holiday specials I've watched ever since I was a kid. Yes, I still watch them, okay? Actually, we all loved them. I mean, seriously. Rudolph! Charlie Brown and the sad little Christmas tree! Frosty the Snowman! Come *on*. You know you love them, too.

16

TODAY, THE ACTORS ALL HAVE the morning off, so Mom is up early and ready to come to breakfast with me. She's oddly quiet, and I wonder if last night's performance was a bust.

"How did it go? Were the Parisians impressed with the show?" I ask casually. Sometimes you can get a person out of a funk by distracting them.

"Hmm?" Mom says as if her mood is a thousand miles away from the play. "Oh, it was fine."

We have a mostly silent breakfast. There are no dares today since Dad told me he doesn't send them when I'm going to be having "bonding" time with Mom. Um, no thanks, and please call it something else that won't make me barf.

It's kind of weird to be at a table alone with Mom again, since I've gotten so used to the other kids. I post my latest pics from last night's cooking class online so Dani and my friends back home can see them. I like how happy we girls all look smooshed on the couch in Madison's suite.

Mom is absorbed in texting someone, punching her touch pad forcefully as if it had keys on it. Finally, she sets her phone down and stands up. "I need a cappuccino. You want anything? Hot chocolate?"

"How about a mocha?" I say recklessly. Maybe mixing stuff up is a good idea.

"No cinnamon, right?" Mom asks.

"Whatever," I say, feeling even more adventurous, but then I catch myself. New foods might be cool and all that, but I don't want to get too crazy. "Yeah, no cinnamon. But whipped cream. And chocolate sprinkles if they have them, please."

There's a long line at the coffee bar, and I scroll through my phone notifications a little more while I'm waiting. I can't help but notice that Mom's cell is right there, a hand's reach away, taunting me, begging me to sneak a peek and see what's got Mom in such a funk. Then, as if it's a sign I can't ignore, her phone buzzes, vibrating on the table. The polite thing to do is turn it off, right? That's normal.

I really should in case it goes again and disturbs—I glance around to see that no one is really close to us—well, in case it disturbs those people way over there.

Besides, I need some intel. I still know next to nothing about Mom and S.T. I've definitely got to seize this opportunity. I glance back up. Mom is inching forward in the coffee bar line. I don't give my conscience any more time to make me feel guilty and dart a hand out to grab Mom's phone, swiping a finger to silence it. The text log is still up, and I see that she's been texting with Nic, the director. It's boring actor talk—things not being quite right with the technical crew, blah blah blah. Nothing newsworthy. But then I see that Mom's been texting a lot with . . . Dad? And, in a separate conversation, of course, S.T.

I sneak a quick look at the coffee line situation. Mom is ordering. I might not have much time. Okay, S.T. it is. This is definitely the right choice, because he's not texting about theater stuff at all. **I really like you, Jocelyn. Ever since the other night, I can't stop thinking**

"Good morning," a voice says, and I drop the phone with a little gasp, looking, I'm sure, even guiltier than I feel. I glance up to see no one else but S.T. himself, smiling smugly at me.

"Your mom around?" he asks.

"Totally." I scramble for the phone, clicking the menu screen and shutting it off. "She's getting coffee."

"Oh, good. I'll wait for her, then." He slides into an empty seat, still with that smug look he can't help having.

"Well, adieu to Paris," he says jovially. "I wanted to thank you for including Kylie in the cooking class last night. She had a really fun time."

"I did, too," I say.

S.T. glances around and then drops his voice to a whisper. "Things have been kind of hard for her lately. She could really, you know, use a friend, and she's wanted to be yours for a long time."

"Really?" I can't hide my astonishment. At both revelations: that chipper, enthusiastic Kylie could be having a hard time and that she really thinks I'm friend-worthy.

"It's good to see you girls connecting," he says sincerely, and that starts pinging my internal alarm. What if this isn't about Kylie at all? I think of the define-the-relationship text I just read. What if this is S.T.'s smarmy way of showing me potential Mom's-new-boyfriend friendliness?

Happily, I see Colby approaching our table with a hopeful-looking Logan—they both are probably looking for Kylie. They arrive as Mom is finishing up in the coffee line.

"What's up, Christa?" Colby says, grabbing a chair and swinging it around to sit on it backward. "How was your girls' night?"

"Really good," I say. "What did you guys do?" The boys tell me about their vid tournament while S.T. stands to intercept Mom for a covert conversation. They're talking in such low voices I can't make anything out, even though I watch them out of the corner of my eye. *Dang.* I stink at gathering intel.

"Later, Todd. Please," Mom says, brushing past him with a bright smile. "Hey, guys." She sets my drink down, her old attention-getting enthusiasm back in place. "I have a great idea. Who's up for a sightseeing cruise down the Seine River?" She waves a brochure at us. "Colby? You want to join? And Logan?"

The Seine sounds nice enough, but I can see S.T. leaning in. "Kylie and I are in."

"Kylie's going, too?" Logan echoes. "Sounds fun."

"Hooray!" Mom says. "The more the merrier."

Merry is not exactly the adjective I would have chosen. But, seriously, what other option do I have? I can't really bail. Besides, time with Mom plus all these other people is going to be way less awkward than time with just Mom. And now that I know from Mom's phone that Something

Big is going on with her and S.T., I desperately need more information. A boat ride will be the perfect opportunity to observe S.T. and Mom's interactions up close.

I stare at them while we wait for Kylie, watching so intently that I realize I've drunk half my mocha without even thinking about it. And it is *so* tasty.

I check my arms. No hives from unknown ingredients. No signs of impending anaphylaxis. My heart rate is normal. I don't even have a smidge of anxiety. What do you know? Across the way, Mom and S.T. are talking like two normal parents whose kids like to hang out—well, make that normal parents for theater bums. Maybe the fact that they've concealed not just the make-out party but the DTR texts and whatever else is going on is proof of what good actors they are.

Later, we all board the long cruise boat by a sturdy-looking metal ramp that leads us directly to a fancy deck area. Part of it is under a clear window roof with toasty space heaters to keep us warm. The rest of the deck is open to the wind and the elements, polished wooden floors leading out to the modern-looking metal railing. Festive greenery wraps around the posts, twirled with little twinkle lights that barely show up since it's daytime. Once we settle in, S.T. and Mom find some deck chairs and park themselves in a corner near a space heater with a tray of little French sandwiches and a bottle of champagne between them. They are talking, but there's not really a way for me to get close enough to eavesdrop. At least not without having to join their conversation, which is so *not* my goal.

Besides, Kylie is telling Colby all about last night. Like every. Single. Detail.

I thought Logan was into Kylie, but he seems more into the boat ride. He's popping back and forth between us and the deck railing like a Ping-Pong ball. I tell myself that's the reason I want to help him out. It's not at all that Colby seems really into his conversation with Kylie. Not one teeny little bit about that.

"Hey, Logan," I say. "Come listen to what we made last night. It sounds way better than your pizza."

"Oh, yeah," Kylie says, switching gears. "But I bet French pizza is beyond good." She launches into a description of our cooking class.

"Phew," Colby says after a minute, when Logan has replaced him as Kylie's audience. "Logan wanted to come on this ride for a chance to talk with her, but it's like she's in a perpetual Logan-free zone."

I look at him skeptically. He seemed pretty pleased with the Logan-free zone.

Colby continues. "I can't tell if she even knows he's alive. Is she into him at all, do you think?"

I glance at Kylie, who is giggling at Logan's goofy expression. "I think Kylie is into all boys," I say without pointing out the very obvious fact that she seems into Colby as well. From somewhere behind me I hear S.T. and Mom's volume escalate a bit, but not enough for me to make out what they're saying. I crane my neck around for another peek.

"What do you keep looking at?" Colby says, following my gaze. "Oh."

Mom and S.T. aren't even paying attention to the champagne. They've leaned in close and are having an intense conversation.

"Well, S.T.'s definitely into *her*, that's for sure," I say. "See how his feet are pointed in toward each other? That's body language for a crush." For some reason I don't want to tell Colby about sneaking looks at my mom's phone. However necessary it was, I feel guilty about it. Like I've been logging on and reading Mom's private email or something.

"What?" Colby says skeptically. "How is that possibly true?"

I shrug. "Ask the editors of *Seventeen*. I don't make up the info, just report it." I'm trying to sound tough, like I'm not all worried about Mom and S.T. hooking up, I'm just an observer gathering intel. I'm on the case.

"What does *Seventeen* say about *that* kind of body language?" Colby asks, nodding toward Mom.

It's her turn to talk. She's hunched over, her hands flying expressively as she talks, her eyebrows making funny little jumps for emphasis.

"Too much coffee," I say with a laugh, but inside I'm bothered by it. If Mom was chill, I wouldn't worry. If she was all superficial and happy, it would be like her normal extra-friendly self. But this is the kind of intense she saves for her real friends, or for those heated conversations with Dad. She obviously feels strongly about whatever she's talking about. Or maybe it's just that she feels strongly about S.T.

The rest of the cruise is kind of a bust. Kylie gets seasick and spends most of the afternoon in the bathroom. Logan hovers nearby with a stash of water bottles. S.T. and Mom finish their über-intense talk, but then they decide to be Present Parents or whatever, and Mom comes to chill with me and Colby while S.T. constantly checks on Kylie. I wonder if Logan is bummed that instead of getting some quality time with the girl he likes, he's hanging with her dad. I'm secretly glad that Colby isn't over there with Logan. Kylie finally emerges and lies down on the deck chair, a damp towel over her eyes.

I try to manipulate things so that I can observe Mom and S.T. in action more. "Do you think Todd needs help?" I ask for the third time.

"What?" Mom sounds annoyed. "Christa, no. He's fine. He's been parenting Kylie for years. Just like I have for you." She gives me a strange look and directs her attention to Colby. "Now what were you saying about that one emergency landing?"

Colby has been sharing all his travel horror stories, and while there are funny parts, they aren't salvaging this train wreck of a trip. Near the end, S.T. pulls Mom aside for another intense conversation, but this time I can barely even see them from where they're standing by the upper deck. The aftereffects, however, are a doozy.

"I have a migraine," Mom says when we get back to our hotel. "Too much shellfish."

"Shellfish are one of the top six allergens," I say automatically. "And the top adult-onset allergy." I peer into her face. "Your eyes are kind of puffy. Do you think you might be having a reaction?"

"Thanks, Dr. Christa," Mom says, waving me away. "It's nothing a trip to the Jacuzzi with a glass of wine won't help."

"Wine has histamine," I say, quoting WebMD and

grabbing my purse. "It will heighten any allergic reaction. I can go to the pharmacy and see if they have some Benadryl. We really should have some on hand anyway." I remember seeing the green neon pharmacy cross on a sign above a shop a few doors down from the hotel. "Or some kind of European version of it. I wonder if they have something dye-free here." Some people are really sensitive to those artificial food colorings.

Mom seems underwhelmed. "Christa, stay here. I'm fine. It's just a headache."

I force myself to stop obsessing over her theoretical shellfish reaction, reminding myself that the first reaction is usually not too severe. But the minute she starts vomiting, I'm calling 911 or whatever it is the French dial for emergencies. I grab a notepad to distract myself and scribble out what I've observed today.

- S.T. is totally into Mom.
- S.T. initiates intense conversations.
- S.T. has really bad breath.
- Mom has a migraine after talking to him; whether that's because of his bad breath or their conversation or the actual shellfish, I'm not sure.
- I feel gross after being on a boat in the wind all day.

It's not exactly illuminating. And then there's the fact that I'm beginning to wonder if I could have an allergic reaction simply by being around so much shellfish. I take a long, hot shower and wrap up in the hotel's fluffy towel afterward and order up two pots of chocolate. Mom is still lying down. I drink both of the chocolates while watching what must be a French Christmas movie followed by a dubbed American one. Mom comes in at the tail end of *Miracle on 34th Street*. And she doesn't have any hives. *Phew.* It's late when we finally go to bed, but chocolate and a movie binge is enough to put me right to sleep.

17

WE'RE HEADED TO LONDON TODAY. I've made it through Florence and Paris without any severe allergic reactions and without having a severe talk with Mom. Maybe the last leg of this trip will also turn out okay. There's a knock on the door. I hope it's not S.T. again.

Fortunately, it's the bellman with a special delivery. "I didn't want you to check out without this being delivered," he says as if he must give a reason for the in-person delivery. I thank him and ignore the fact that he seems to be lingering for a tip. I mean, am I supposed to tip or not? But since I'm out of euros and don't want to wake Mom, I just shut the door, cementing, I'm sure, his impression of me as a bratty, rude American.

I'm surprised Dad has sent something since usually

our travel days are dare-free. The package is the smallest one yet, and its wrapping paper is not Christmassy at all. It looks like plated armor, which is what I feel like I'm going to need to wear when I read the candy-cane-striped gift tag for #8: DARE YOU TO RIDE THE CHUNNEL TRAIN.

My heart rate speeds into panic mode just reading the word *Chunnel*. I mean, if there is *anything* worse than being trapped in a metal tube flying through the air, it's definitely being trapped in a metal tube hundreds of feet underwater. Is Dad CRAZY?

Inside the little box is a key chain holding a flashlight shaped like a train and a little silver placard engraved with the saying: *You can do anything you set your mind to.* He *is* crazy. I don't need the guidebook to know what the Chunnel train is, but I do grab my itinerary. Yep. Just like I remembered. We have a choice between a longer train ride and a ferry across the water or the much quicker Chunnel route. I had already decided on the first, thankyouverymuch. I want to live.

Besides, it's really kind of pushing my luck to even think about doing the Chunnel. I've somehow survived flying across the Atlantic and trying new weird foods, but I don't want to tempt fate. I know it will mean not fully completing the Christmas scavenger hunt, which is something

I've never ever done in my life, but, come on, risking your life shouldn't be a dare. Besides, I know this is really Dad's lame attempt to "help me grow."

When I was little, Dad would come up and sit in the chair in my room until I fell asleep, because I was so afraid of the dark. Now, of course, I can go to sleep without a light on and everything. Well, without a real light on—my cell display doesn't count, okay? But I still hate dark, unknown places. Whenever we drive through tunnels on the highway back home, I feel the old, tight, scared feeling return. Dad always tells me: Breathe in—you can do anything—breathe out—you set your mind to. I guess it's some meditation technique. I can't tell if it works or not, but I do it anyway in the tunnels. Except that tunnels are like ten seconds long, not a whole two and a half hours. The Chunnel is the perfect place for some horror survival movie. Or an awful hijacking terrorist plot. Or a disaster of epic proportions. Or all of the above. I grab my phone.

I can't do the Chunnel, Dad, I text him. **I'm sorry.** I forget that it's the middle of the night back home, so it's a few minutes before his reply comes.

Chris, there's nothing to be sorry about. The dares aren't meant to make you feel bad but to give you a chance to embrace the unexpected. Look at how far they've

brought you already. I know you can handle the Chunnel— you can do anything you set your mind to. But if you decide to take the ferry, that's fine too. Just promise me that you'll be on the lookout for the unexpected there too.

I'm not going to lie. I'm relieved that I got an official pass on the dare. I pack my suitcase, but I keep stumbling across that little key-chain flashlight. It's taunting me with the fact that no matter what reassuring things Dad says in his text, I still won't have done one dare.

A minuscule voice inside tells me how good it might feel to do something I'm afraid of and come out on the other side. The tunnels on the highway are like that—all racing heart and sweaty palms during them—but the best feeling once I'm out. It's kind of euphoric. Maybe I could do the Chunnel. I did survive the cooking class, after all. I feel the anxiety build inside while I finish packing and go down to breakfast, but I also feel something else: the teensiest bit of determination, and I already know what I'm going to end up choosing.

"Mom," I say when we're at the table together. "I think I want to do the Chunnel train."

Mom sets her phone aside. "Seriously?" The expression on her face is not exactly giving me a confidence boost. "You know that you can't get off once you're on. You stay in the train the whole time."

"I know," I say, clenching the little flashlight in my hand so hard that it hurts my palm. "But I want to do it."

"I'm behind you one hundred percent," Mom says. She knows how I feel about tunnels. She doesn't tell me to do the breath thing when we're driving together, but she does crank up the music and try to distract me with car dancing. That sometimes works.

"I'm kind of sad to leave Paris," Mom says. "This trip is going by so fast." She looks at me and sighs. "And we've had so little time together."

I mumble a response. Now that the decision is made, I'm seriously distracted by what it means that I'm going to have to actually go through the Chunnel. I don't even listen in on their conversation when S.T. comes over to the table and joins us. Or respond when he tells us that they are planning on taking the Chunnel route, too. Whatever. I don't even care. I have to put my surveillance on hold. It's not compatible with fighting anxiety anyway. This could be my last day on earth, and if it is I might as well be nice to people like S.T. and Kylie. And Colby. It's a relief when he joins us.

"I love the Chunnel train," he says when he finds out our plans. "Can I sit with you guys? It's kind of boring to go alone, and Dad has already flown to London to deal with the tech crew."

"Of course!" Mom says, exchanging looks with S.T., which I think is parental code for "Nic is such a bad dad for leaving his kid alone in Paris." That might be true, I guess, but Colby seems to have turned out okay and doesn't seem to be bothered by it at all.

Soon, we are all checked out of the hotel and taxied over to the Chunnel boarding area. "Your mom says you're kind of claustrophobic," Colby says while we're waiting in line to get on the train.

Thanks, Mom. Well, it's not like I'm going to be able to hide it if I'm sitting next to Colby. "Just a little nervous," I say between breaths. The deep breathing thing works because it keeps you from hyperventilating, which I know from WebMD is bad because it ramps up your fight-or-flight response. Mine is always ramped up anyway, and extra is absolutely no bueno. And, yes, I know I read too many health articles on the internet. "I mean, it's underwater." I have to talk in short bursts, because the deep breathing thing keeps me from real conversations.

"Gotcha," Colby says, giving my shoulder a friendly squeeze.

"Thanks." I examine my palm and the now likely

permanent train outline branded there.

"It's really going to be fine, you know."

And it is, at first. The Chunnel train isn't as cramped as an airplane, which is helpful, and it has big windows on each side. Colby and I find a seat together behind Mom and S.T. I guess everyone has opted for riding the Chunnel train, because Logan and Owen sit down in the seats across from us. Their parents are somewhere a few rows up, near Kylie and Sasha. Which must be enough distance that Logan feels like he can ask me about Kylie.

"Do you think she likes me?" Logan asks as the train crew prepares to depart. The attendant has begun to review the safety procedures, and I can't believe that Logan thinks *now* is a good time for relationship advice. Seriously. Which is more important? Some dumb she-loves-me-she-loves-me-not conversation? Or knowing where the emergency exits are?

I crane my head around to see where the attendant is pointing. It seems like some of the windows might become exits if needed. "I don't know," I tell Logan absently. All my senses are on overdrive, and I feel hyperalert and jumpy. Exiting underwater seems even stupider than exiting at thirty thousand feet. "Why don't you just ask Kylie?"

"Maybe you could send a note," Colby suggests as the

train crawls forward and then begins to pick up speed, sending my heart rate skyrocketing along with it.

"Why a note?" Owen pushes his glasses up on his nose. "Why keep it a secret? If you like someone, you should just tell them. Didn't you learn anything from Ron and Hermione?"

Logan rolls his eyes at Owen and turns to me. "Christa, you're a girl."

"I'm glad you noticed," I say, eyeing the elderly man who is seated next to the nearest exit window. Could he really help in an emergency? He looks kind of weak.

Logan keeps going. "A note or a talk. Which is better?"

"It doesn't matter," I say before working in another long breath. "If you like someone, you should tell them how you feel." The train makes a strange clunking sound, and I grip the armrests hard. "Don't let your fears hold you back," I squeak, saying it to myself as much as to him, but I'm not sure it's working. My fear seems to be winning. My body is still on high alert, and I have a panicky moment where I feel like I might pass out, which could possibly be the Worst Thing Ever. Passing out in front of everyone. Having to have EMTs carry me somewhere else on the train, and what exactly do they do if someone needs emergency treatment? What if the peanut-allergy girl from my school ate peanuts underwater on a train? I play out several worst-case scenarios involving swelling and epinephrine and death, which seems to drain the rest of my adrenaline.

Through it all, the train still chugs along, taking us out of France and into the quiet darkness that tells me we must now be underwater. People are laughing and chatting and looking at their phones. Some are even sleeping. Owen is reading out loud from the final Harry Potter fight scene. My anxiety is fading into the background, leaving me feeling really, surprisingly fine . . . as long as I don't think about the fact that I'm hundreds of feet under the water. As long as I don't imagine being confined somewhere with no way out. As long as I don't think about how someone up there is eating a snack that smells suspiciously peanutlike, and, seriously, how have I not checked WebMD to see if you can get an anaphylactic reaction from smelling something? As long as . . .

CLUNK.

That is definitely not a normal train noise. I take it all back. I still have adrenaline left. Lots of it. And it shoots up, sending everything in me into panic mode.

CLUNK. CLUNK. CLUNK. Louder this time. And then the train stops. Hard. The passengers' volume increases. Even Owen looks up from Harry Potter 5. Then the emergency lights come on. *Oh no. We are so going to die.* I knew it! I knew I shouldn't have done this stupid dare! Note to future Christa: Never, ever, ever travel underwater. Humans weren't made to be underwater.

A voice comes over the intercom, but it's in French, and all I can understand is *s'il vous plaît*, which I know means "please." Would they really be using good manners if they were telling us to brace ourselves for The End? Please what? Please prepare to die?

Finally, it switches to English, where a calm-sounding woman reassures us that nothing is wrong, but a maintenance issue has come to the attention of the crew and we will need to stop for a few moments for repairs. She asks us to please remain in our seats. Which is like the worst advice ever. In disaster movies they *say* to do that when really you are wasting the few precious minutes that are the only opportunity to load into the *Titanic* lifeboats or whatever in order to save yourself.

"Repairs?" I hiss to Colby. "Like the train is broken? Or the tunnel is leaking?" I lost my breathing rhythm somewhere back around the time of the first clunk.

"Are you okay, honey?" Mom turns around. "Try not to worry. Everything is fine. I bet this happens all the time."

"You've ridden the train before." I say it to Colby like an accusation. "Has this ever happened to you?"

"Well," he stalls. "Not exactly."

"It is *so* not fine, Mom." I'm having to work hard for breaths, and I feel all dizzy and weird. It's going to happen. Not only are we most definitely going to die down here, but first I'm going to pass out on the train. Or maybe go into anaphylactic shock. I *did* have a granola bar a few minutes ago. Maybe I've suddenly become allergic to oats and—I need to get out of here, like *now*.

"My hands," I whisper. "I can't really feel my hands." They've gone all numb with needle pokes like when your foot falls asleep, and the same thing is happening around my mouth. Probably from the allergic reaction.

"I think you're hyperventilating," a voice says, and I see that S.T. and Mom are up and hovering near my seat.

Awesome. Dr. Todd is on the case. "No," I manage. "It's the oats. I'm allergic." I try to bend my fingers, but they are stiff and unmoving.

S.T. looks at Mom for confirmation, but she shakes her head, looking confused.

"Breathe deeply," S.T. says, "from your belly." He leans closer to help, and I feel like I'm going to lose it. It's so crowded already, and if I have to smell his bad breath . . .

"Leave me alone, Todd!" I shout, pushing him away. I guess I mean it more as a dying gasp, but it comes out really loud and really angry.

"Christa!" Mom says in a horrified voice.

I can't even process what she says next. I can feel my throat closing up. I am so going to die. Right now. In the Chunnel. And Mom wants me to care about my tone of voice?

"Please go away," I gasp out. "I don't want your help. Or Todd's." I find that talking makes the choking feeling lessen. "Why don't you two just have another long talk or go make out somewhere or whatever it is you're so busy doing and LEAVE ME ALONE!" There. That cleared my airways.

"Christa!" Mom's face has gone all red. She turns to Todd. "I'm so sorry. She's upset. It's anxiety."

"It's okay." S.T. turns away. "I should probably check on Kylie anyway."

Colby squirts some water on a napkin before handing the bottle to me. "Have a drink. And put this here." He places the cold cloth on the back of my neck, and I feel a little calmer. Taking a few sips forces me to breathe a little slower, and I can feel the panic washing away in waves. My hands are shaky. And very, very cold. As my head clears, I don't think I'm going to die anymore.

"Everything okay here, madame?" An attendant comes up behind my mom, eyeing me. "We've had some complaints. About shouting."

Heat fills my body, chasing away the cold. So maybe there could be something worse than passing out in the Chunnel train. Causing a huge scene for no reason at all. I realize the people in the rows around me are staring. Even Owen and Logan are gaping at me. When they see me looking, they both grab for the Harry Potter book, studying it as if it were the manual for repairing the train.

"I'm sorry," I say in a very small voice. "I'm okay. I just panicked. That's all."

"Claustrophobia," Mom says, smiling at the attendant, but after he leaves, the smile disappears.

"Christa, honestly. You have got to pull yourself together and get this under control." The lines in her forehead ease the teensiest bit. "I'm sorry you are having such a hard time, but really, to shout at Todd like that." She sighs heavily. "I'm going to find a piece of fruit for you. Get your blood sugar up. Maybe that will help."

She moves away, shaking her head, but I see her stop up the aisle, not by a train attendant but by S.T. Figures.

"How are you doing?" Colby says in a quiet voice.

"Panic attacks suck."

"A panic attack?" I say slowly. "You think that's what that was?"

"Don't you?" Colby squeezes my shoulder. "They eventually pass, but man, it's the worst feeling. Like you're going to die."

I crunch the plastic water bottle in and out, watching the liquid level inside rise and fall. *A panic attack.* I guess that's statistically way more likely than random-onset anaphylaxis. I suddenly feel very, very stupid.

"You know what I always do?" Colby is saying. "To get my mind off it?"

"Always?" I echo. "Like, you've had a lot of them?" Colby always seems so laid-back, like nothing can frighten him.

"Before I lived with my dad, I used to be alone with my mom a lot. And it wasn't good." He pauses. "It was scary."

"Yeah," I say. "The world is kind of scary." If that was a panic attack, I can't imagine how awful it would be to have one with no one around to help.

"One time it was really bad, so I—" He pauses, sheepishly picking at a fingrernail. "Wait. Do you really want to hear this?"

"I do." My curiosity is piqued. Both about Colby's

tactics for dealing with panic and about this side of him I've never seen. "What did you do?"

"Well," he says. "We had this old atlas, and I would get it out and spread it on the floor and plan all the trips I was going to take around the world." He laughs. "It was really out of date, so some of the countries don't even exist anymore, but it was like a portal to another place. By the time I'd figured out all my trips, the panic would be gone." He reaches into an inside pocket of his jacket and pulls out a crumpled world map. "So. Where should we go today?"

I'm trying not to stare at Colby, so I look at the well-worn map.

"Well," I say in a shaky voice. "Iceland has always sounded pretty cool to me."

"Excellent choice." He puts a little penciled star by Iceland. "Famed for its natural beauty and excellent seafood."

"I hate seafood, but I'll take the natural beauty."

"Okay, then an adventure tour it is." He taps a finger on the map. "After Iceland we need to go somewhere warm. Sri Lanka, I think." We spread the map on the little table between us, and I barely notice when a bing comes through on the intercom announcing that the repairs are complete and we will be continuing on our journey to London. Our imaginary trip around the world takes us the rest of the way to England. When we're almost there, Kylie and Sasha plop down in Mom and S.T.'s empty seats.

Kylie twists around to face me. "They're talking."

"Who?" I say kind of absently, because I'm thinking about the best route from Casablanca to Abu Dhabi.

"Your mom and my dad." For the first time I see Kylie frowning.

"Oh. Right." And I suddenly have the realization that Kylie might have some feelings about all of this, too. I know, I know, I'm mega self-absorbed for not realizing it sooner.

Kylie looks back at me, and for a minute I see some of the same unsettledness I feel inside written on her face, but she doesn't say anything else, and I don't know how to ask her if she's happy about S.T. and Mom or upset, because if she's upset it would mean she doesn't like Mom, and as mad at Mom as I am right now, she's Mom, and how could Kylie possibly not like her?

Since the girls have joined us, Colby folds up the map. "We'll have to finish our trip later," he says in a quiet voice. "Besides, we'll be in London soon."

"I wonder if the queen is in residence," Sasha says, explaining that you can tell by the kind of flag flying over Buckingham Palace. "It would be so cool to see her."

"Or Prince Harry," Kylie says with a squeal, snapping out of her momentary negativity and replacing it with her usual fangirling.

But I think Owen might be the most excited about this part of the tour. He's got a whole list of Harry Potter dreams to fulfill, and he starts reciting every one of them the rest of the way there. When the train finally stops, I can hardly believe that I've made it. Through the sea. Through a panic attack. Through that Harry Potter read-aloud. And out the other side. As Colby hands me my bag, which he's pulled down from the overhead compartment, I realize that I don't know how I would have made it through the Chunnel Repair Fiasco without his around-the-world trick, and that he somehow did it without making me feel stupid.

"Thank you," I say as I take the bag.

"No prob," he says with his trademark half smile.

"No. I mean, *thank you*. For everything."

He looks down like he's the one who's embarrassed. "You're welcome."

As we leave the Chunnel train, I'm beginning to realize that Colby might not just be a good friend. He might be becoming one of my best friends.

18

WHEN I REJOIN MOM, HER face looks as tight as if she's just been Botoxed or something. She hands me a small orange, but I don't eat it. The thought of Mom going to some secret compartment on the Chunnel for a Botox treatment plants in my mind, and I can't get the ridiculous picture out of my head. Especially when I imagine S.T. in the chair next to her. I'm so worn out from the anxiety that I feel a bit loopy and choke back one of those impossible-to-stop laughs.

Mom notices. "We are not done talking about your behavior, young lady."

I stop laughing. Oh, yeah. Me losing my mind in a panic attack and blurting everything out means that Mom *knows* that I know they were making out.

I successfully avoid any personal interaction with Mom all the way to our hotel and through check-in and distract myself with just how brilliant London is. And, even better, London is totally dressed for Christmas. There are green wreaths and twinkling fairy lights on all the buildings. The wet streets glisten, reflecting back all the city's sparkle. Even Big Ben is lit up with red and green. Our hotel is, of course, perfection, and I'm happy to see that this time my part of the suite is actually a tiny little separate room with its own twin bed.

Of course I still have to pass Mom as we're getting our things unpacked, and it's beyond awkward. Mom talks in her extra-quiet whispery voice that she usually only uses the day after she doesn't get a callback for an audition. I try to be as invisible as possible, saying yes or no politely whenever we have to interact.

The lucky thing is that since it's Christmas week, Mom has extra performances on the front end, and all our free time on the back end, which means even less time avoiding each other than in Paris. If we can make it through tonight, I should be pretty awkward-talk-free for the next few days. Mom claims the bathroom for a long tub soak, which is perfect for me, and not just because I'm dodging her. I am so wiped from today it's like all I want to do is crawl under the covers and sleep for ages. Or just the one night. Whatevs.

My ninth dare arrives bright and early the next morning. After conquering the Chunnel and having a good night of sleep, I feel like I can do anything Dad's possibly thought up, which maybe was the point of him daring me to do the Chunnel, I guess. No extra bravery is needed today, however, because this dare is *shopping*! There's a little snowman gift tag that reads: **#9: DARE YOU TO BRING HARRODS CHEER TO THE PALACE GUARDS.** The extra instructions are quite long, because they include these little educational printouts about wassailing and mumming, which I guess are old British holiday traditions. Basically, the dare involves me making an idiot of myself, of course. But it does *not* involve enclosed spaces or flying or underwater travel or new foods. So—yay!

We're already scheduled to go shopping at Harrods that morning before going to Buckingham Palace. We have to take the Tube to get there, which is not awesome, because, well, metal tube way underground. No escape. But at least there's no water or flying involved, right?

I have a tiny flicker of nervousness when we first squish on the train, which is crowded with commuters and tourists, but it evaporates once Colby and I start people-watching.

There's a lady so plugged into her device that she doesn't notice the cute guy next to her checking her out. And a grandma bribing two kids in a double stroller with what she calls "biscuits" but look like plain old cookies to me. And Owen, who is fully decked out in Gryffindor colors in honor of Harry Potter.

The ride doesn't take long, and soon we are all headed up the escalator straight into the store. And, look, I'm not trying to be sexist or anything, but clearly the girls are *way* more excited about this stop than the boys. There are floors and floors of displays—stuff from all over the world. Harrods' motto is seriously "All things for all people, everywhere." You can even buy a ten-thousand-dollar box of chocolates or a freakin' diamond manicure in this department store.

The Christmas-decoration floor (literally called Christmas World) is like the North Pole on steroids. Fake snow. Christmas trees of all colors—lavender seems to be "in" this year—and lights and music galore. I wrap some silvery tinsel around my neck like a scarf and flit from tree to tree, picking up ornaments until I'm covered with glitter. There are whole walls of gift wrap and ribbons, decorations for fireplaces and bedrooms and bathrooms and any kind of room you could possibly imagine. I move on to the little Christmas villages, where tiny people are going about their daily business dusted in fake snow. I want to live in one of those villages. No. I want to live on this floor.

The dare tells me to bring holiday cheer to the guards, which means that I have to set the scene with some decorations. I plan a strategic route that takes me around the edges of Christmas World and then up and down each aisle so I don't miss anything. Once I've seen everything, I decide to go classic for the dare. I settle on holly and ivy with little twinkling lights and Santa hats for all of us. I haven't told the other kids about the dares yet, but it's not like I can wassail or whatever incognito this time. Besides, after everything we've done together and been through, I actually want them to know about the dares and join in on them.

Next, we stop by the food hall, which has samples from practically everywhere in the world. I avoid the suspicious-looking ones, because I'm not feeling *that* good, and instead I gorge on the plain chocolates that the salespeople are practically forcing into our hands. Finally, I buy a tin of biscuits and some Turkish delight, because, hello, England? Narnia? Christmas? And finish it all up with a thermos of black tea the saleslady says is their most popular.

On the way to Buckingham Palace I tell the others

about how my dad and I do scavenger hunts together every year and explain each of the different dares he sent in Florence and Paris. As I talk, I realize that it's not just that I want to tell them about the dares, but that they really want to hear from me, almost like . . . wait for it . . . we all feel like we're actually friends. "So this next one is a mini-performance to share Christmas cheer with the guards at Buckingham Palace, and I could really use your help." I fill them in on the details.

"The guards are trained not to respond to anyone or anything," Madison says with a smile. "I think you'll find them a tough audience."

"It's not about what they do in response," Kylie says. "But about giving them some holiday cheer. They don't have to respond for it to be worth it."

"Exactly," I say, grinning back at her. Kylie gets it.

"The queen *is* in residence after all," Sasha says, pointing at the royal flag waving crisply in the gray overcast sky. Buckingham Palace looms in royal finery behind its thick wrought-iron gate. There are huge evergreen wreaths hung from the brick gateposts, and the guards are, as expected, stoically standing at attention. Tourists sidle up alongside for photos, and soon, M&M have parked us in front of one of them.

"Go for it." Miles folds his arms and grins at Madison as though he's settling in for a fun show.

"O-kay," I say. "Let's have everybody do something different." I look at my dad's list. "Colby, what if you sing the wassailing song first? And, Logan, maybe you've got some parkour or break-dancing moves to go along with it?"

"Absolutely." Logan lunges down into a runner's stretch.

"Owen and Sasha—do you guys want to prep the snacks?"

"Sure," Sasha says. "And then I think I might try to do some caricatures of the guards to give them as presents."

"Oooh, good idea!"

"Brilliant," Owen says in his fake British accent. "Accio cookies . . . er, biscuits, rather."

Now, on to Kylie and me. "What's left?" she asks.

"This poem," I say, showing her the poem my dad sent called "An Old Time Christmas." "Do you want to take turns with each stanza?"

"Super!" She gives me a warm smile.

Once everyone knows what they are doing, we put Operation Holiday Cheer into action. I play "Here We Come A-wassailing" on my phone, and Colby sings along, dramatically acting it out with exaggerated movements.

Logan completes an impressive impromptu set of hand-spring jumps far enough back from the palace gate that he doesn't get into trouble. By the time he's done, a little crowd of tourists has gathered, joining M&M as our audience.

"We are here to bring you Christmas cheer!" I say when the boys have finished their performance. "We know you can't respond, but we figure it must get kind of boring standing here all day, so . . . enjoy!"

We have enough biscuits to give some to the children watching, which Owen does with a flourish. Sasha has found a spot off to one side to sketch, and I can see by the expressions on the faces of the people peering over her shoulder that she's doing a good job.

"We'll leave some refreshments here for you for when you change shifts," I say before Kylie and I launch into the poem. I'm surprised at how good Kylie is. All of us are theater kids, so it's not like we've never had walk-on roles in our parents' plays or whatever, but she's, like, really, really good. I tell her so when we're done.

"Thanks," she says, looking for the first time a little uncomfortable. "This is so fun, Christa."

She's right. We finish our performance with another round of singing, this time all joining in together on "We

Wish You a Merry Christmas." We leave the rest of the treats and keep singing as we head off to explore nearby St. James's Park.

"Logan really wants to do something cool for Kylie before the trip is over," Colby says as the group splinters off into pairs. Owen and Sasha are walking up with M&M, and Logan is more than happy to be with Kylie.

"He wants to know if we'd kind of hang out with them when he does it," Colby continues. "So it won't be so awkward, you know? Keep it kind of chill."

"Um, sure," I say. I haven't really noticed Colby talking to Kylie a lot or anything lately, but if he's still into her, he seems pretty okay with Logan's interest. "I guess so. But I don't think it will be awkward. Kylie seems like she might go for him."

"I guess we'll see." Colby shrugs. I can't tell if his tone means: "we'll see, and if she doesn't, I'll make a move," or if it means he's indifferent. "I think Owen's advice the other day was good. You know"—he swallows hard—"if someone likes someone else, they should just tell them, right?"

"Right," I say, but I keep my voice carefully neutral. That squirmy feeling inside is back, and I wonder if he's talking about himself and working up the guts to tell Kylie how he feels. I realize that I really, really don't want to encourage him to do that. Just then, Kylie sort of slips and Logan catches her, and it isn't really that funny, but I'd do just about anything to change the subject before Colby asks me to help him get Kylie's attention or something, so I laugh, too long and too loud. Colby gives me a thoughtful look, but it works, and he drops the subject. And, even though I really like hanging out with Colby, I'm kind of glad when we catch up with the others, who have broken back into a rousing rendition of "We Wish You a Merry Christmas," which carries us all the way to our next destination.

19

WHEN I WAKE UP THE next morning, Mom's already gone for her early call time. If my luck holds, maybe I'll never actually have to talk to Mom about S.T., the Chunnel, or why things are so weird between us. Okay, so maybe we *do* need to talk eventually, but not now. Instead, I focus on the small envelope the bellman delivers to my door. For the first time, there aren't any special props or extra instructions inside, just a gift tag with stockings by a fireplace that reads: #10: DARE YOU TO WALK IN SOMEONE ELSE'S SHOES. It's all very mysterious, and I wonder if Dad has finally made a mistake in his organizational masterpiece. What am I supposed to do? How will I know if I've done it? I think about texting him but have a sneaking suspicion that part of the dare is figuring it out. I decide that I will try to spot opportunities to "walk in someone else's shoes" (I so hope it's not meant to be taken literally) all throughout the day and then see what Dad has to say when I text him later tonight.

I'm done with breakfast in record time, so I go to the library, which is our new group meeting place. The others aren't there yet, but Madison is curled up on a comfy couch sipping a cup of tea by the crackling fire. She sets the novel she's reading aside when she sees me approach. "You're an early bird this morning."

"Are you here every morning?" I ask.

She nods. "I like to start my day off with some quiet. Helps keep me centered. Besides, it's hard to put down a good book, you know?"

I don't really know. I like books all right, and I've even found some good ones, but—and I know this is super controversial and everything—in my opinion, the movie is always better. I settle in on the other end of the couch, holding the to-go cup of hot chocolate I've brought from the breakfast room. It's weird to see Madison doing normal-person things, kind of like when you run into your teacher in the grocery store on a Saturday morning. I know teachers have *lives* and everything, but it's always startling to discover them sporting yoga pants and sloppy hair. It's the same with Madison. She's supposed to be clipboard-bossy-icebreaker-slumber-party organizational queen. And here she is . . . reading *Pride and Prejudice*. I've seen the super-long BBC version of it with Mom, and it's actually not too boring.

"Lizzie is my favorite," I say, nodding toward the book.

"Of course!" Madison says, with a little flair. "Though part of me envies Jane a little bit, too. What would it be like to be so *good*?"

A laugh escapes before I can stop it. "But you do everything right. Madison, you already *are* Jane."

Madison waves my objection away. "Doing things right isn't the same as being good and kind. *And* peaceful. Jane always seems so peaceful." Her smile looks a little wistful as she says it, and it makes me wonder what Madison is really feeling behind all of her clipboard control.

We talk about the book (well, movie for me) until the rest of the kids get there, and when Madison swaps her novel for her clipboard and puts on her tour guide role again as she runs through all the things we are going to see today, she somehow looks different, less bossy and overbearing and more earnest and extra conscientious. Dad might have been right—she really is a good tour guide. As I follow the other kids to the bus, I feel pretty good about the morning. It's barely nine o'clock, and I think I might have already accomplished today's dare.

We spend the morning at Westminster Abbey. I know I say that basically every sight we visit is amazing (because, Europe!), but the Abbey seriously is. To me, it looks a little bit more like a palace than a church, with its soaring spires and sprawling grounds. The exterior is breathtaking, especially with its huge decorated Christmas tree by the entrance, and the interior even more so.

There's a service going on when we enter, so we have to slink around quietly for our self-guided tour. It's kind of cool, actually, because there are candles lit in the dim corners and the air smells like spicy incense. There's a big nativity scene set up near the front, and we stop by it to listen to the people chant-singing things back and forth to each other. The clear music echoes throughout the main chamber. As a result, this church doesn't have that heavy quiet some of the others did, but it does make me feel tucked away and hidden in a world of beauty and age. The Abbey has been around for something like a thousand years. Kings and queens have been coronated here. Famous authors like Lewis Carroll and C. S. Lewis have been memorialized here. I even point out Jane Austen's tablet to Madison, and we have a super-silent fangirl moment together. Great artists and architects have worked here. Political scheming has happened here. Every stone crackles with history, and I'm kind of sad when Miles rounds us all up to tell us it's time to go.

"I have a surprise for you for lunch today," Madison tells us as we come outside into the bright daylight, and I feel like crawling back and hiding in a corner of the Abbey. Food plus surprise is never a good thing. I pop in my ear-buds and pick my calmest playlist. Maybe if I, as Madison said this morning, find some quiet, I can deal with this food surprise thing.

The others don't seem fazed at all. Logan is, of course, literally bouncing off the walls and curbs as we go, with Owen and Kylie flitting around him. Colby and Sasha seem to be having a thoughtful conversation, and occasionally Colby looks back at me. Once he even waves me over, but I shrug and point exaggeratingly to my earbuds. I've been quasi-avoiding Colby since last night, because I'm secretly worried he'll tell me how much he likes Kylie, and then what will I do? I try not to think about it, and soon we arrive at an unimpressive modern building with a whole line of women queued (as the British would say) outside.

"We aren't just eating lunch, we're preparing it and serving it, too," Madison says, taking us in a side door and introducing us to a stout older British lady named Lois. Soon, I see what she means. Lois and other volunteers from the Abbey run a soup kitchen that feeds people who don't have homes.

"We serve around three hundred women a day," Lois says, handing us all gloves, aprons, and (ugh!) hairnets. "We have forty-five minutes to get the food ready, and then an hour or so to feed everyone. I'll need you to pay attention, do as you're told, and enjoy yourselves!"

Once we're inside the big industrial kitchen, Lois quickly assigns each of us a task. Every step of the meal prep is organized and planned, down to the minute the hot food is supposed to come out of the oven and into the heated serving trays. I volunteer to cut up green and red bell peppers (which are happily on my safe-foods list) for the fajitas that we're making. Next to me, Owen starts chopping onions, which has to be the worst job, since his eyes get all red and watery almost instantly. I try to ignore the fact that Colby offers to grill chicken with Kylie, and they seem to be having a lot of fun figuring out how to use the long tongs to flip each piece until it's browned just right. Sasha and Logan set to work mixing up a tasty-looking salsa, and Madison and Miles begin preparing quarts of bright orange juice that the Brits call squash. Other volunteers are sprinkled throughout the kitchen, and Lois oversees it all, weaving through her worker bees like a queen with a hairnet and a wooden spoon. I do the same thing over and over—cut off the pepper tops, dig out those little seeds, and slice and dump the strips into the bin. I lose myself in the rhythm of the work. By the end of it, I think I know what Madison meant about centering one's self in quiet.

Lois's voice breaks into my Zen mood. "We're right on schedule." Except she says it the British way with a *sh* sound. "Time to serve." The other volunteers show us where to put food on the serving line, give each of us a big utensil, and station us behind the steaming trays. With a flourish, Lois rolls up the partition dividing the kitchen from the dining room, which is decorated with little paper Christmas ornaments hanging from the ceiling tiles over empty round tables.

Once we're all set, the ladies enter and begin filing through the serving line. I'm not sure who I expected to see. I guess if you had told me we would be chilling with the homeless today, I would have thought of the not-so-clean people who sit under the awnings of Chicago buildings, hands outstretched for money. And there are some unkempt women for sure, wearing padded layers of clothing and smelling sour, but others look ordinary. Like if I had passed them in the street, I would have thought they were just like anyone else. Some are old, with white hair and wrinkled skin. Others are young, maybe only a handful of years older than me. I try my best to put the salsa I'm scooping on a blank spot on everyone's plate. I know I hate it when unknown foods touch each other. Once we've served everyone, Doris encourages us to fill our own plates and go join the women.

"We don't just offer nourishment for the body, we nourish the soul as well. Go make some friends."

I select safe foods—a little of the peppers I've chopped, some plain chicken, and a tortilla—before making my way toward the dining tables. I feel shy and out of place, and then one of the gray-haired women waves me over. "Looking for a spot, lovey?" she says in a thick British accent. "Right here. Come sit next to Granny Doris." She pats an empty chair next to her, and I slide onto it with a smile.

"That all you eating?" Granny Doris says when she sees my plate. "Got to fatten you up, lovey." It's weird to be called lovey, but I kind of like it the way she says it. The other ladies at our table are older as well, and some of them seem to know each other.

I take a bite of my chicken and ask Granny Doris how she's doing today.

"Never better, lovey, never better. Every moment is a blessing, after all. Every day is full of gifts the Good Lord sends us to unwrap," she says with a smile. "I've got a full stomach, a table of friends, and it's Christmastime. Nothing like a holiday to cheer up the spirits." She tells me how she's been staying at a shelter near here for the past six months, ever since her only son died and she's been left on her own. "But I wouldn't have met these precious ladies back in my old neighborhood, that's for sure." She gestures to the other women at the table. "I've made so many new friends, you wouldn't believe it!"

That's not the only thing it's hard for me to believe. How can this woman who's lost so much still be so cheerful and brave about life? As the other ladies talk, I learn that they all have challenges. One lost her flat (American translation: apartment) after something went wrong during her back surgery and she couldn't work anymore. Another is a recovering drug addict and trying to stick with her first job in years. I listen to their stories, and my own problems seem way smaller. I mean, I've never had to wonder where I would sleep at night. Or stand in line for food. Or, for that matter, had no choice about what I was going to eat. Don't get me wrong, I'm not going to go all crazy and eat loads of unknown ingredients or anything, but it does make me look a little differently at the carefully partitioned food on my plate.

I glance up to see Madison gesturing to me from the front of the room. She and Miles are gathering together the other kids, which I guess means that the meal is over. I wait for a pause in the conversation and then thank the other women for such a nice lunch. "I've got to go, but I'm really glad to have met you all," I say sincerely.

"Now aren't you the one with good manners?" Granny Doris leans over and gives me a side hug. "I'm the one who should be thanking you. You brightened up our table today, didn't she, girls? You, Ms. Christa, are one of God's gifts today." It's the sort of thing I'd roll my eyes at if anyone but Granny Doris was saying it. Somehow, this woman with the powdery skin and watery blue eyes has some sort of hidden secret joy, whatever her circumstances. I don't believe she's faking herself out with a positive attitude or made-up compliments. She means what she says, and her kind words make me feel all warm inside. I wonder what it would be like to live with that kind of optimism, to dance toward life expecting gifts in every moment—even ones with hard things—instead of being fearful of everything that might go wrong.

Back in the kitchen, there's not really time for

philosophizing. Lois assigns jobs again, and this time I find myself on one side of the huge stainless sink, scrubbing pots next to Kylie.

"Can you believe what some of those women have gone through?" Kylie says, elbows deep in sudsy water as she fishes out greasy serving utensils.

"No," I say, aiming a squirt of soap at the big pan I'm working on. "What I don't get is how they've dealt with such hard things and still are . . . well . . . happy."

"I know, right?" Kylie swishes some tongs in the water, sending soap bubbles scattering. "Maybe part of growing up is learning how to do that, how to celebrate the good things even when everything seems to be going wrong."

I stop my scrubbing and study Kylie. What she said was totally deep. Apparently the soup kitchen brings out profound thoughts.

"I want to learn how to do that," I say carefully. Maybe it's being here, or maybe it's the fact that I now actually consider Kylie a sort-of-almost-not-so-annoying-after-all friend. "It sucks when things you don't want to happen happen, and there's nothing you can do about it. But it's even suckier to feel all depressed and worried about it."

She stops washing the ladle in her hand. "My dad told me about your parents' divorce. I'm really sorry."

The flash of irritation I feel at the thought of S.T. talking about *my* family fades when I see how Kylie is looking at me—not with her usual Kylie exuberance. Or with pity. But with eyes that actually make me feel like she sees me, like she understands.

"Yeah," I say, trying to laugh away the tears that are stinging the backs of my eyes. "Divorce is the worst."

"Tell me about it," Kylie says. "My parents split up two years ago, and I'm still not used to it."

"Does it"—I fidget with the scrubber sponge, squeezing water out and then soaping it up again—"does it ever get easier?"

"Not easier. It just changes." Kylie reaches for the overhead nozzle and begins to rinse her dishes. "For a long time I just wanted things to go back to the way they used to be. Then, little by little, I began to see that things could still be good, even if they were really different." She props up the utensils in the drying rack, studying them and making a point of not looking at me. "The weirdest part was when my dad started dating other women. It was like it felt really *real* then, you know?"

"Oh, I know," I say, thinking about that awful surprise-y feeling I had when I stumbled upon S.T. and Mom. Something in my tone must give me away, because Kylie breathes a huge sigh of relief.

"You *know* know, don't you? That there might be something going on with our parents? I mean, how weird is that?"

"*Totally weird,*" I say, relieved to not have to break the news to Kylie. I realize by her expression that I might sound a little too weirded out by it all, so I backpedal a bit. "Not that your dad isn't super nice or anything, it's just . . ." I trail off, not sure what to say.

"That you've never seen your mom *dating* anyone, right?" Kylie laughs. "It was so bizarre the first time Mom asked me to help her pick out an outfit for a guy she wanted to impress. I was all, 'How do I avoid this entire conversation?'"

"*Exactly* how I feel ninety-nine point nine percent of the time!" I grin, looking at Kylie with new appreciation. So we may never be besties or anything, but there's a lot more to her than I once thought. I suppose I never bothered to look past all the giggles and über-excited selfies to realize that she is a person just like me. I mean, *duh,* of course she is. But I see now that judging her based on those few characteristics isn't exactly fair. Kind of like someone thinking all I'm about is weird food hang-ups and panic attack moments. Or me looking at a homeless person and seeing only rumpled clothes and empty hands.

Later, when I'm back at the hotel, I realize that, whether Dad meant it to be or not, all of today has been about completing the dare. From seeing Madison as more than a bossy walking clipboard to meeting the extraordinary Granny Doris to, perhaps most surprising of all, stumbling upon a potential kindred spirit in Kylie, I've learned to listen to people's stories—walk in their shoes, as Dad dared me—and to really see them. Definitely unexpected, and definitely worth it.

20

I WAKE UP ENERGIZED BY my new optimism. If today is a gift, I wonder what it will bring me. Like in the symbolic, Granny Doris sense, you know? Because I also get to open a literal present, since today is a dare day. And literal presents are most definitely worth getting excited about, too. This morning's package is wrapped in shiny silver paper. There's nothing inside but a gift tag with fancy ornaments on it and the message: #11: DARE YOU TO TRY ON YOUR CROWN AND JEWELS AT THE TOWER OF LONDON.

I read about the famous old prison in the guidebook, especially the part about how the crown jewels are kept under armed guard. I doubt that even one of Dad's special behind-the-scenes passes can get us a chance to try them on. His instructions don't say much except that I should go to the tower with Mom and ask to speak to a guard named Jane. For once Dad seems not to have checked the itinerary very closely, because Mom has already left and is in rehearsal all day today, and I'm supposed to go with M&M to the Tower with the other kids. Which is okay with me, because things still haven't really thawed between me and Mom.

As if on cue, just then I hear a key card in the lock, and Mom comes in.

"Forget something?" I say, twisting my hair up into a bun. I have half an hour before I have to meet the others and was looking forward to having the suite all to myself.

"No," Mom says, sitting on the little sofa between our rooms. "Chris, we have to talk."

Uh-oh. "About what?" I try to keep my voice neutral, but Mom's not falling for it.

"I think you know." She sighs and kicks off her shoes as if she's settling in for a long chat.

Double uh-oh.

"Chris, you've been avoiding me for days." She raises her eyebrows when I open my mouth to protest. "Don't deny it. Not to mention how you behaved on the Chunnel train."

"How I behaved?" I manage. I get it if Mom calls me out for being distant or whatever, but the Chunnel was like life or death. "I had a panic attack. It was scary." My hair is so not behaving. I take it all down and start again.

"Not that. When you shouted at Todd." Mom frowns. "And me." She shakes her head. "I don't get it, Chris. This is the trip of a lifetime. It was supposed to be our great adventure, you know"—she gives me a strained smile—"our special bonding time together. But your attitude stinks. And we've hardly spent any time together."

I *can't* believe she just said "bonding time." All the good feelings and Granny-Dorisyness of the morning disappear like a puff of smoke. "We spent time together in Paris." Ugh. No matter how many times I rewrap my bun it keeps getting these bumpy parts on the top.

"With Colby," Mom says flatly. "I know when you're avoiding me, Christa. It's like some days you're a completely different person."

Okay, this is getting ridiculous. "*I'm* a different person?" I look at her in the mirror as I'm trying to get the elastic around my stupid bun. "You're the one who's changed *everything*."

"What's that supposed to mean?"

I rip the rubber band out and shake my head vigorously.

Forget the bun. "Oh, I don't know: new apartment, new routine, new plans for Christmas?" I rake my brush through my hair, ripping at the tangles.

"Christa." Mom sounds dismayed. "I thought you wanted to come on this trip."

My eyes are watering now I'm brushing so hard. "It's not the stupid trip!" I shout.

"See?" Mom stands and folds her arms. "That's exactly what I'm talking about. So many kids your age would be beyond thrilled to be in Europe, and all you do is grump around."

"That's not true." I clench my jaw as the brush snags on a huge knot.

"You'll ruin your hair if you do that."

I slam the brush down on the dresser. "You know all about ruining things, don't you?"

"Enough," Mom says.

"No. It's not," I say. I'm not shouting anymore. I'm keeping my voice deadly calm. "You're the one who's done enough, Mom. If it wasn't for you, we'd be home in Chicago—not at your apartment—but with Dad. All of us. Together." I'm shoving things into my bag as I talk. "Or Dad would be *here* with us. Instead of our family being all jumbled up like it is." I zip the zipper and look up at her through my tears, which is when I realize that my stinging eyes have turned into a full-on ugly cry. "And Todd? I *saw* you making out with him, Mom. I *know* you're seeing him. And lying to me about it."

Mom's mouth is set in a thin line, but her eyes are watery and red.

I keep going. "You may think I'm grumpy or whatever, but I'm not the one who tore our family apart. You've done that. *You're* the one who's done enough."

I sling my bag over my shoulder and beeline for the door, smearing my palms across my wet cheeks.

"Chris . . . ," Mom says in a strangled voice, but I don't let her finish.

"I have to meet the others." And the door between us slams shut.

It takes me ten minutes in the lobby bathroom to pull it together. My mascara hasn't run but my eyes look all puffy, and I don't want people to know I've been crying. My hair is still a disaster, but I pull it back into a bad-hair-day pony, wishing for the first time that I could wear Madison's yellow visor to cover it up. So much for being all optimistic about today. I'm not sure even Granny Doris could find the gift in having a big fight with Mom followed by the ugly cry. I can't think too much about what just happened or my tears start firing up again, so instead I focus on Dani's text messages. So much has been going on since the Chunnel ride that I've kind of neglected her, and I take some time to respond to her, avoiding any that ask about "Jocelyn's hottie."

Soon, I'm ready enough to meet the others. I'm too late for breakfast, of course, which isn't a huge loss since the Brits seem to think fish and tomatoes are an acceptable food first thing in the morning. *Ew.*

Once I'm on the bus with the others and snarfing down two granola bars I feel better. Mom might skip rehearsal today, but there's no way she'll skip the performance tonight. She'll definitely be gone when we get back this afternoon, and I'll make sure to be asleep when she comes home. If Mom thought I was avoiding her before, I'm about to take it to the next level.

"You're quiet today," Colby says as we get off the bus in front of the Tower of London.

"Meh," I say, brushing the whole morning off. "I'm okay." Which of course isn't true. Whenever I think of how Mom is upset with me I feel all hard inside. I can't believe *she* is the one acting all hurt. I shove the jagged little feelings and the constant replay of our fight out of my thoughts and try to focus on the day ahead.

It helps that everyone is all relaxed and BFF-ish with one another now, but the tragic thing is that this means they've all succumbed to Owen's infatuated-with-England ridiculousness and are practicing horrible fake British accents. Which is really embarrassing once we leave the bus and are out in public.

"Oi!" Owen shouts. "Birds!"

"Brilliant!" Logan says, which is really the only Britishism he's landed on. Kylie just giggles.

We've driven by the Tower of London at night, when it's lit up with red and white lights for Christmas. But in the day, it's all pale yellow stone and stark shadows. Madison gathers us together to tell us an old English legend that says the ravens living at the Tower of London protect the crown and the country. "If the ravens leave," Madison explains, "it means that England will be lost."

I'm not buying the legend, but we join the other tourists, who are throwing bits of bread to the famous birds. One catches a piece of bread midflight.

"Smashing," Owen says.

"So." Madison comes up to me, but she's talking in her normal American accent, of course. "Ready for your dare?"

"Right-o," I say, sounding more Australian than anything. "Wait. How did you know?"

"The eleventh dare is today, isn't it?" Miles says from her other side.

"Yup." Madison looks up from the clipboard she's consulting. "Dare eleven. Tower Jewels."

I tear off a huge chunk of bread and throw it at the biggest raven, who caws and flaps out of the way. I knew that Dad had people helping him with the dares, but M&M have just confirmed that they know all the details of all the dares. I think of how Mom skipped rehearsal on the one day the dare included her. *Mom* probably knows all about them, too. I feel five years old inside for thinking that this was somehow a Big Secret between only me and Dad.

"Well, you've done a good job with the dares," I say weakly, because M&M are still standing there waiting for me to respond. "Thank you."

"Seriously, Christa," Colby says as we file in after the others. "Is everything okay?"

The last thing I want is some kind of heart-to-heart with Colby. First the fight with my mom and now the realization that I've been all secretive when Mom really knew all along. "I'm fine," I snap.

A hurt look flickers across Colby's face, but he hides it well.

"I can't wait to see the torture chambers in the

dungeons," I say brightly, hoping we can keep the conversation light from here on out. You know, by focusing on cruel and unusual punishments. And dying.

Colby rolls with it, though some of our old camaraderie feels forced. There is a special tour guide called a yeoman who is going to be taking us through the Tower. He is full of dates and names and old stories of prisoners kept here as we pass through the thick bleached walls surrounding the tower and make our way through the maze of inner courtyards. There are lots of other tourists, and when we finally arrive at the crown jewel exhibit, it's super crowded. They keep the actual jewels here, so there are a ton of guards, and we have to go through these crazy steel vault doors with electronic beams. It's *so* cool.

Inside, there are more than just crowns. There are weapons and scepters, garments and all kinds of jewelry. After I've had a good look at all the loot, I decide that if I'm going to do the dare, I should probably try to find somebody named Jane like the dare said. I hesitate. Does it count if I do the dare in a different way? Mom's not here, and now I know her participation was part of Dad's plan, but I'm not going to wait for things to get better with Mom, because, I mean, the way things are going we'll probably be all the way back to Chicago before *that* happens. Besides, I'm *so* close to completing the whole scavenger hunt!

"Ready for your dare?" Madison asks. "Come this way."

"Ooooh!" Kylie says. "You're doing a dare here? Can we come?" Sasha overhears, and they both want to know the specifics.

"Sure," I say as Madison takes me out of the room and to a guard who looks more relaxed than the others. "Is there someone here named Jane?"

The guard reappears with a woman who smiles at me and then looks at the other two girls. "Wasn't there just supposed to be two of you?"

Argh! Is *everything* going to remind me of the Big Fight?

"There's been a change of plans."

"Okay." Jane shrugs. "Come with me."

She takes us past the vault and down a corridor to what looks like it must be the guards' break room. Hanging over the lockers are two dress bags.

"Ohmigosh," Kylie says in a near whisper. "This is *so* cool."

I unzip the first bag and see a gorgeous silvery-purple dress just my size. A pretty snowflake necklace dangles from the hanger with a paper crown wrapped around it. A note is pinned to the front, but I decide to read it later. I'm a little parented out for right now.

"That's beautiful," Sasha breathes.

"Can I?" Kylie asks, her hand hovering over what must be Mom's dress.

"Go ahead," I say. Inside is a long velvet black dress and matching necklace.

"Wow," Sasha says. "Your dad is so cool."

"The paper crowns are worn at Christmas dinner here in Britain," Jane says. She explains how crackers, which are kind of like little popper fireworks, are also part of the traditional dinner.

"Ohmigosh, you are so lucky," Kylie says.

I think about what having dinner alone with Mom is going to be like now, and I don't feel very lucky. When we return to the group with the dress bags hung over our shoulders, the boys want to know all about the dare.

"I'm not sure what else it involves," I say, "but there are fancy dresses. And paper crowns. And crackers."

"Can I see?" Owen asks, holding the foil-wrapped cylinder in his palm as if *it* were a jewel. "I've always wondered what these were like. Harry and Ron get them at Hogwarts's Christmas dinner, you know."

"We know," Logan says, rolling his eyes.

When we go back to the bus for the lunch break, I stow

the dresses in the baggage closet, wishing I could tuck the mess with Mom away just as easily. The rest of the afternoon is full of sightseeing, and for the most part I'm able to distract myself from the Big Fight and join in.

Later, when I'm back in the suite, I flop Mom's dress bag on her bed. I wonder if I should hang it up, but then I wonder if Mom will see it in the closet, and if she doesn't she might ask me about it, which would mean having to talk to each other. Besides, this dare is already kind of ruined with her not actually being there or anything, so I leave it where it is to make sure she sees it.

I do unzip mine and try it on. The dress is so pretty, like a little sliver of moonlight wrapped around me. I put on the dainty necklace and study the result in the mirror. My hair is still a disaster, of course, but I like how the rest of me looks. This is the most grown-up dress I've ever had. I open the little envelope pinned to the front and read Dad's note:

> Chris, I'm so proud of you for how brave you've been. And not just with the dares. I know we've had a lot of changes this year, and when changes come it can be easy to hide from them or keep everything the same. But I know the real Christa loves adventure and is up for any challenge. I'm so glad you've allowed

the unexpected to take you places you were always meant to go. Now get all fancied up and go out and celebrate! I've made reservations for you and your mom at Galvin at Windows so you can have a fancy feast on Christmas Day. Don't forget to wear your crowns.

I toss the note down. I will not cry. I will *not* do the ugly cry. Especially not in *this* dress, the one I'll probably never get to wear, at least not anytime soon. I can't imagine going anywhere for Christmas dinner, not *now*. Not with Mom.

I wonder if Dad would be as proud of me if he knew about the Big Fight this morning. The fact is that I'm *not* brave. I *hate* change. (Hello, granola bars and plain cheese pizza.)

I slip off the dress and hang it carefully back in its cover before crawling under the blankets. I wish I could redo this whole day. Even better, every day since November first.

I'm still lying there awake when Mom gets back from her performance. I hear her quiet movements about the suite and then the crinkle of the dress bag and the sound of the zipper.

I wonder if she's reading the note Dad pinned to her

dress. I wonder what he wrote to her. Or if she feels as awful as I do.

"Chris?" Mom's voice is low and hesitant. "You awake?"

I don't say anything. I'm afraid that if I do she'll be able to tell I've been crying, and I just cannot handle more crying or another Big Fight or anything else today. I flip over on my side, giving her my back, and pull the covers up higher.

"Chris, I'm sorry. I shouldn't have lost my temper earlier." There's a long pause, and Mom continues. "I didn't know you were feeling all, well, all *that* about the divorce." I hear the bed creak as Mom sits down on the end. "I know it's been hard on you, and it's really normal for you to feel upset with all the changes." She laughs. "*I'm* upset with all the changes, too."

I squirm a bit under the covers. I feel that tight, angry spot inside of me melting the teensiest bit.

"We haven't always gotten to do things just you and me." Mom's voice sounds a little sad. "I know you have a lot of special memories with your dad—the scavenger hunts and everything—and that you're busy with your friends. And those are really good things." She pauses. "But I was hoping this once you would choose me, that this trip could be one of *our* special memories." She gives a sharp little laugh. "I guess I was pretty blind. I know theater is not really your thing, but I was thinking that if you came to a performance, we could bond over it or something. Like we did about art." She sighs and stands, her weight lifting off the bed. "Maybe we can start over tomorrow, okay? I'll try to listen more. And talk less."

"Okay," I mumble to the covers, because I can get that much out without crying. The room gets quiet after that. It's a weird moment when you discover that grown-ups maybe don't have everything figured out. I had thought that Mom was all fine with the divorce and happy with her new life, but it kind of sounds like she's confused, too, and possibly a little scared as well.

I lie in bed for a long time. I hear Mom come in after her bath and get ready for sleep. I hear the sounds of London outside and how they grow quieter the later—or earlier in the morning—it gets. I lie there listening to the silence until I finally fall into a restless sleep.

21

I WAKE UP SUPER EARLY, because I had one of those too-real dreams. I sit in the little chair by the desk and replay it all: the way Mom forgot to pick me up from band camp (since when have I *ever* dreamed about band camp?) and I'm so upset with her that I stand there and yell at her and she doesn't say anything. She just looks at me all silent and sad. *Ugh*. Not so subtle, Subconscious Christa. The sour feeling from the dream mixes with the memory of our awful fight and the heavy weight of things being all screwed up between me and Mom, so when the bellman finally delivers today's package with an uncertain smile, I realize that I am scowling and in super-grump mode. I paste a grin on, which must be even more disturbing, because the bellman scurries off without lingering for a tip.

Today's dare is wrapped up in an envelope with a thick red ribbon twined around it. Attached is a gift tag with a pile of presents scattered on it that reads: "Happy Christmas Eve!" and I stare at that for a minute. Christmas Eve. Which definitely should be a happy day. The lead-up to my favorite day of the year. But, like everything else, it feels messed up and wrong. Underneath the message is a fancy #12. The twelfth dare. The finish line. The end of this year's scavenger hunt. And the reminder that in a few days I really will be home again.

There's a note attached that says I'm supposed to Skype Dad before I open it. I hunt around our suite for the laptop, which I can't find, so I check Mom's room, which is uncharacteristically empty. That's when I hear Mom's voice from the bathroom, and I inch closer to eavesdrop. I know, I know, it's not cool to listen in on other people's conversations, but would you really do anything differently if you were in my situation? Desperate times, people.

I can tell that she's talking to someone, and after a while I figure out it's Dad, which explains the missing laptop. I bet she's Skyping him.

"I tried," Mom is saying. "But she's been all obsessed with the dares you sent." Then comes the muffled sound of Dad's voice, but Mom interrupts him before I can make out what he's saying.

"I *know*, Adam." That's Mom's super-annoyed voice. "I know that you wanted her to feel connected to home. I get it, okay? But *I* wanted to have something with Christa, too. I wanted her to have something *new*, okay? I just feel like I'm screwing this up so much." I feel a little guilty. I didn't know Mom felt like she was the one making mistakes. I keep listening.

"And it's not like Christa is being charming either," Mom says with a sigh that makes me bristle. "I honestly don't know what to do at this point. You have no idea how hard this is."

Hard for whom? For her? She has *got* to be kidding me. So Mom is confiding in Dad, and apparently he knows all about the Big Fight, at least her side of it. I wonder if S.T. knows as well, and the thought of him turns me from grump mode into serious angry mode, like subconscious Christa has emerged from the band-camp dream and is ready to pick up where she left off with Mom. Mom is acting like *she's* the one who's having the hardest time.

"You know how she gets," Mom is saying. "It's drama-queen central in here."

Oh no she didn't. I don't stop to think, and I wrench open the bathroom door, sending Mom popping up from the edge of the bathtub, her mouth making a surprised little "o" when she sees me. Behind her, I can see the laptop screen, which shows Dad sitting in our living room, wearing his old tattered flannel robe.

"Christa?" he says, peering at the screen.

"Yeah, it's me. Your daughter. The one you've been *discussing*." I take a step closer so that Dad can see me as well as Mom, and I turn to face her. She has no idea how drama queen I can be. "I guess it's taken so much time to tell Dad how *difficult* I've been that you haven't had a chance to fill him in on what else you've been doing, huh? Why don't you tell him the truth, Mom? Why don't you tell him about S.T.?"

"S.T.?" Mom looks confused. "Christa, what are you talking about?"

"*TODD?*" I shout. "You know, the one you've been *in love* with?"

"Christa!" Mom says, but I don't let her talk. I turn to the screen.

"If she won't tell you, I will. You think Todd's a nice guy. Well, it turns out he's trying to get Mom. He sent her flowers and everything, *and* they spend all this time together." With each detail I expect Dad to look sad. Or shocked. Or regretful. Or *something*! But he's just sitting there patiently, listening and nodding as if I were telling him about my latest sightseeing trip. "Maybe they were spending time together before the divorce, for all I know." I turn to Mom. "Is *Todd* the reason you wanted a divorce? I mean, I knew you were behind it all along, but was it because you were *cheating*?"

"That's enough, Christa," Mom says in a tone that's supposed to let me know I'm in dangerous territory. Like I care.

I focus back on the laptop. "Don't you get it, Dad? Todd is interested in Mom, like interested in *dating* her."

"Yeah, Christa, he is," Mom interrupts. "And you know why we haven't started dating?" She folds her arms. "Because I was worried it might be too soon *after* the divorce."

No way is she making me feel guilty over the Todd thing. "But he even texted you to say that—"

"You've read my texts?" Mom doesn't look surprised anymore. She looks pissed. "No matter what I say or do, I'm the bad guy here. I've tried and tried on this trip, Christa, but all you've done is shut me out. You've avoided me and done just about everything you could to get out of coming to see the play and even more to escape spending time alone with me. I know you're upset, Chris, but I have feelings, too, you know."

"Oh, I know all about your feelings," I say. Okay, so I'm

basically shouting at this point. "And why does everything have to be about you and your play?"

Mom shakes her head and says quietly, "I give up. Adam, you deal with this." And she leaves the bathroom in dramatic tears.

I am *so* not kidding. It's like a theater stage exit. Somebody cue the sad background music. Except I'm not exactly feeling sad for Mom.

"Chris," Dad says from the laptop. "Sit down. Take a deep breath, sweetie. I can see you're really upset."

I breathe in, and when I exhale, it's as though all the anger seeps out of me like a leaky balloon. Which leaves me wanting a good cry followed by crawling back under the covers and staying there all day. Or, even better, doing both at the same time.

"Look, sweetie," Dad is saying. "I know how hard this has been on you. I hate that you are struggling with the divorce so much."

Usually Dad knows just the right thing to say to make me feel better, but that is *so* not it. Why do people always say "I know how you are feeling" when they can't possibly know? Has Dad ever been a thirteen-year-old girl stuck in Europe with her newly divorced mom, who is now starting to date other people? Has Dad ever seen his mom making out with some other guy? Has Dad ever been called a drama queen? If he has, then we have way, way more important things to discuss.

But Dad keeps going, and it only gets worse. "What you have to understand," Dad is saying, "is that it's hard on me and your mom as well. You also need to know that you've got some information wrong. *I'm* the one who wanted the divorce in the first place. *I'm* the one who thought that things weren't working anymore. It wasn't because of Todd at all."

Wait. *Dad* wanted the divorce? That can't be true. I open my mouth to argue, but Dad cuts me off.

"No, it's my turn to talk now, sweetie. *I* sent your mom the flowers, because I was so proud of her for finally pursuing her dreams."

No wonder the little flower tag had Dad's nickname for Mom on it.

"And, yes, I know about Todd. He isn't the enemy here. He's a good guy, and you're right, he wants to date your mom. But, sweetie, you've been jumping to conclusions."

Everything inside turns up another degree. If he *sweeties* me one more time, I might explode.

"You know why that hasn't happened yet? Your mom has been worried it's too soon for you, Chris."

He pauses as if to let his words sink in. They do, but

not in the way he hopes. Is that supposed to make me feel better? That Mom is going to blame *me* for not getting to be with Todd?

"I'm happy for your mom," Dad continues. "I'm glad that she's got this new touring opportunity and is meeting new people who bring her joy. I hope that you can have that same thing, too, Chris. It's part of why Mom and I planned these dares for you, so that you could find some of that spark again and learn how to rediscover the things you love."

Dad has more to say: about how he's been worried about me, how he and Mom just want what's best for me, and the always-being-a-loving-family thing again, but I'm *so* not listening carefully anymore. I feel totally ganged up on. Dad is on Mom's side. And Mom has helped Dad plan the dares. Mom and Dad have been plotting how to make me *better*, like some kind of emotional intervention? And S.T.? How can S.T. *not* be the problem? I feel confused and ambushed and hurt and angry and all mixed up inside.

"I know your mom was really hoping for some special one-on-one time with you. It might be hard for you to be excited about it, but I wonder if you could make more of an effort. You know, try to make some time to see her show while it's in London. And then maybe go out for dessert afterward, just the two of you."

"All right!" I say before he can go on about Mom anymore. "Enough with the play already! I'm going to see it tonight, okay?" I hadn't officially decided that until just now, but, whatever. Anything to make this conversation stop. My head hurts, and I feel stupid for all the things I've gotten wrong and guilty for accusing Mom of what Dad already knew, and awful for shouting at both of them, and everything is so messed up that I don't even know what else I'm feeling on top of it.

"Okay," Dad says in a quiet voice. "One more thing—"

But thankfully I don't have to hear the one more thing, because just then the Wi-Fi goes on the fritz, and our Skype chat blinks off. Perfect timing. I snap the laptop shut and sit staring at it for a minute. I so don't want to have to go out into the hotel room to see Mom. I frown at myself in the mirror. I have total bedhead, and my eyes are puffy. I guess I've been crying without even realizing it. I wash my face and wet down my hair, taking a long time to do it.

After a while I notice that it's super quiet out there, like empty-room quiet. I peek my head out and find that I have the suite to myself. I've been hanging out in the bathroom for nothing. I grab my phone and send Dad a quick text: **Wi-Fi fritzed out. Sorry. Talk to you later.**

The last thing I want is for him to blame me for basically hanging up on him. I'm already in enough trouble as it is.

Now that the Skype chat is done, I find my anger has gone as well. Instead of being all mad, I feel kind of hurt that I've been so out of the loop with my parents. And like a complete jerk-face daughter. My feelings aren't so mysterious anymore. Did I really just throw that tantrum in the bathroom? Did I really say all those horrible things? I know that all of this means some kind of parent-daughter heart-to-heart later on, and I'm not sure how I feel about that. I debate burrowing under the covers and going back to sleep, but I know that will only mean I'll be here this afternoon when Mom gets back. Besides, today is the very last day of the kid tour. As upset as I am, I don't want to miss out on that.

I go back to the bathroom and tackle my hair. Then I give reflection Christa some advice. "You've got to pull it together, Chris." If I get all focused on the drama with my parents, I'll end up with more of the ugly cry, or inevitably I'll say more idiotic things to make it worse. I finally tame my hair into a respectable sock bun and put on some makeup to hide the puffiness. "So stuff with Mom and Dad sucks. You've still got a normal life to live. Go on the tour. Go to the play tonight. Figure out the rest later." Maybe going to Mom's play can be some sort of peace offering.

I take one last look at myself in the mirror. "Find the gifts of today," I say, channeling Granny Doris. Which, given how I'm feeling, will be a small miracle.

22

BY THE TIME I JOIN the other kids in the library, my pep talk has worn off. Everyone else is super hyped up, because it's the last day of our tour, and all the itinerary says is: *Special Destination—A Winter Surprise.* But I'm too stressed about the parent thing to even think about the stress of a surprise. I *hate* fighting with my parents. I try to suck up some of the positive energy of everyone else in the room.

"What's the surprise?" Kylie is nearly exploding with smiles. Even Sasha looks a little excited. Madison has put Miles in charge, and he lays out the day's plans in his usual chill fashion.

"You're going to need your warmest clothes. Scarves, hats, sweaters, gloves if you've got them. And extra socks."

"Get your cold weather gear pronto!" Madison says.

"We've got some partying to do."

We grab lunch together at a greasy fish and chips place (just chips for me), before we arrive at the Special Destination. When I finally see what the big surprise is, I'm glad I've brought my scarf and my sweater and my puffy jacket. Even though it's not that cold outside, we've arrived at an outdoor ice-skating rink.

"Welcome to the Frostival," Miles says with a grin. "Ice-skating, a winter market, shopping, and games, whatever your heart desires." He explains that we can do what we want, as long as we stay in the Frostival area. "Meet back here at five p.m. That way we'll have enough time to get back to the hotel so anyone who wants to go to the play tonight will have time to change."

I'm relieved that seeing the play is unofficially part of today's itinerary. It will be way easier to see it with some of my friends beside me, and since it's the very last performance, it's my last shot at making good on my promise to Mom. However upset I am with my parents, not seeing the play would most definitely make things worse.

We start with skating, which I'm actually good at. Dani and I go to the outdoor rink almost every winter in Chicago, so I'm super comfortable on the ice. Some of the others, however, are not. Okay, so only Colby is struggling.

"I've never been," he confesses to me after his third

time wiping out. He gets to his feet, toes pointing crazily inward and legs all out at a weird angle.

"Here," I say. "Let me help." I grab both of his hands and tug him away from the wall he's clinging to like a lifesaver. Yeah, I can skate backward. No big deal. Okay, it's super cool, and it took me two whole winters to learn how to do it. "First you've got to stop crouching over like that," I tell Colby. "Straighten up your legs. And"—I shake his arms playfully—"*relax*. When you're all stiff like that you're setting yourself up for a fall."

We slowly make our way forward, letting Owen and Logan whiz by us with a "Way to go, Colby!" but I can't tell if it's sarcastic or encouraging. The girls are a little better. Kylie swishes past us with a sympathetic smile, and Sasha pretends to ignore Colby's unsteadiness altogether, which is actually helpful.

"You're doing great," I tell Colby.

"Right," he says with a laugh. "For a two-year-old." He makes jokes about his lack of coordination, but he doesn't seem too bothered by his inability to skate. In fact, together, we make a pretty good team. I get to practice my backward skating, and he, well, he doesn't break his arm or anything. We make our way around the rink a couple of times before deciding to stop for hot chocolate.

"Logan's making his move today," Colby tells me once

we're situated on a bench with our drinks. The others are still skating, and Logan is literally doing rings around Kylie. I wonder if she even suspects he's into her. Or that Colby might be, too. People can be so oblivious sometimes.

"I've helped him plan it," Colby explains, "but he's super nervous and sort of hoping you'll get in on it, too."

"Okay," I say slowly, peering at Colby. He doesn't seem at all bothered by the fact that Logan might edge him out with Kylie. "What do I have to do?"

"Oh, just hang with us. To make it seem more normal and everything." Colby fidgets with the little paper wrapping on his cup. It's weird, but I'd almost say that *he* seems really nervous about something.

"We have to set up a few things first, so maybe you girls could go to the winter market together. Then it will seem all chill when we run into you later on."

"Sure." I take the lid off my cup and lick the whipped cream. "But what about Sasha? Can she come, too?"

"Naw," Colby says. "She's already planning to do some afternoon sketching. Owen knows what we're doing. He's brought his book, so I think he's cool to hang out on his own." He takes a big gulp of cocoa. "And before you ask about them, Madison and Miles know all about it. No sneaking off or anything. We'll be right here at the Frostival the whole time."

I hadn't actually thought about that part. Madison and Miles are sitting over on one of the ice-skating-rink benches, both of them glued to their phones. I get the feeling that they're glad to have made it to the finish line of the kid tour without any major catastrophes. It's like they've already checked out.

"Sounds good. So when do I have to get Kylie to the market?"

Colby looks at his phone to check the time. "In about half an hour."

Kylie doesn't take much convincing to come with me. Soon, we are making our way through the different stalls, and I can't help but think that, except for the British accents all around us, I could almost imagine I'm at the annual Christmas market in Chicago. Which, I'm surprised to say, makes me happy rather than homesick, because I'm actually having a really nice time with Kylie.

We stop at a candy booth and buy huge peppermint-flavored striped lollipops, slowly savoring them as we window-shop through the different arts and crafts on display. Maybe it's the magic of the Frostival, or maybe it's that I've eaten so much sugar that I've lost my better judgment, but I find myself slowly leaking out the details of yesterday's Big Fight and this morning's follow-up to Kylie. I tell her about Dad's Skype intervention and how

I'm worried I hurt Mom's feelings and how angry I am at them, and also how angry I am at myself. Kylie's actually a really good listener. She nods and makes sympathetic noises and rolls her eyes at my parents at the right parts.

"I mean, I know they aren't actually trying to screw our family up, but it seems that way sometimes. They're the grown-ups, after all."

"Yeah," Kylie says in a quiet voice. "I think sometimes divorce just feels that way to everyone, like it's not the way it's supposed to be, you know?"

"I guess." What she's saying makes sense. Divorce *isn't* the way it's supposed to be. Who gets married hoping that it's not going to work out? "But it's the way it is."

"I know," Kylie says. "And it sucks. I was so angry when my parents split up. They aren't friends anymore. When Mom drops me off at Dad's she doesn't even come inside. It was awful at first." She crinkles the plastic wrap farther down to reveal more of her lollipop. "But it does get better. Different, for sure, but better." She sighs. "What really helped me was going to this group therapy thing with other kids whose parents had divorced. It was nice having people who understood, you know?"

"I know," I say, giving her a side hug. "Thanks for listening, Kylie."

"Anytime," she says, with a hint of her old perkiness.

"You need to vent? Shoot me an angry text. You want to cry? I can hand you tissues. You want to gross out at thinking of our parents actually *dating*? I'm there."

"Ugh. No thanks to the last one. Seeing them kissing was enough to gross me out for a lifetime."

"Ohmigosh!" Kylie's eyes grow huge. "You saw them kiss?"

I laugh and fill her in. "I wonder if things will actually work out between your dad and my mom."

Kylie shrugs. "Who knows? But it's not like worrying about it will change anything."

I nod, slowly digesting her words. She's right. I should know. After all the worrying I've done this year, a billion things would be different if worrying actually changed anything.

"Besides"—Kylie looks down at her lollipop—"maybe it wouldn't be so bad if they got together. The side perk is *we'd* get to hang out more."

"Good point," I say. I like Kylie's perspective. Maybe I'll make that my new family motto: different, but not terrible. Between that and Granny Doris's advice to look for the day's gifts, I might become an optimist after all.

23

LOGAN AND COLBY FIND US over near this weird performance-art thing where mimes are pretending to be snowmen or people trapped in ice or, actually, I have no idea what they're pretending to be.

"Thanks for rescuing us," I say when I see them coming over.

"Whoa," Kylie says to me under her breath. "They look good." She's not talking about the mimes.

The boys have changed clothes. Logan's wearing this black asymmetrical hoodie with skinny jeans. Colby's got on a cool motorcycle jacket, and he's done something different with his rumpled hair. My stomach does a little flip at the sight of him, and I toss my candy in the trash. The sugar is definitely going to my head.

"You guys ready for an adventure?" Logan asks, and I can tell he's nervous.

"Um, yeah!" Kylie says with a giggle.

"Right this way," Colby says with a flourish. They lead us through the market, circling around back to the ice-skating rink before finally landing at the foot of the London Eye.

In front of us, a huge Ferris wheel–like structure stretches up and over the river Thames behind it. I've seen the London Eye as we've been driving around the city, but up close it's even more humongo, the little glassed-in compartments stretching high up to the top of the wheel. Since it's winter, someone has decked out each one with wicked-looking icicles and twinkling white Christmas lights.

"Seriously?" Kylie squeals. "Ohmigosh, this is going to be great!"

"Great," I echo, because the boys are looking at me now. "Totally."

While we stand in line, Colby turns to me. "Is this okay, Christa? With your claustrophobia and everything?"

It's sweet of him to ask, but what does he expect me to do? Bail on the whole Kylie-Logan project just because I might be a little nervous?

"I'm not sure," I say truthfully. The panic feelings

haven't kicked in yet, but the London Eye definitely checks all the boxes for stress. It's not an airplane. Or the Chunnel train. Or the Tube. But it's still kind of scary to think of swinging away up there in a tiny box.

"I'm good," I say, deciding that I want it to be true. I'm tired of being afraid of everything, of the way I can't even order a new coffee drink without stressing about it. I want to be like Kylie, excited at the prospect of riding up in this famous landmark, not calculating how far out I'd have to jump in order to dive into the Thames from one of those glass cars in the event of an emergency.

We shuffle slowly through the line, watching groups of people cram into each car, until it's our turn to board. I feel my anxiety rising as I wonder how many people are going to squish into our compartment. I see Colby slip a wad of bills to the operator.

"I called earlier," Colby said. "For the special tour."

"Right," the operator says with a wink. "Go on ahead."

I climb inside, following Logan and Kylie over to the big wooden bench placed in the middle. The domed glass walls bubble out to the side, making the space feel surprisingly large, even more so when the operator shuts the door and I realize that no one else is joining us.

"Wait," Kylie says. "It's just us?"

"Yep," Logan says with a grin.

"Well, us and some of the best food." Colby pulls two picnic baskets out from under the bench with a flourish. I'm not so sure about the whole food thing, but I can't focus on that now. The London Eye begins to move, inching upward so slowly that I almost don't even notice we're ascending. I take a deep, slow breath. Maybe this isn't going to be so bad. The whole city sprawls below us, crowding in on the rippling river Thames. It's an absolutely breathtaking view.

"Did you know anything about this?" Kylie leans in to whisper. The boys are busy unfolding tablecloths and unpacking the hampers.

"Maybe," I say, and then come clean. "Okay, yeah, I did, but you've got to have already noticed, right? Logan is mega into you."

"He is?" Kylie looks genuinely surprised, and then really pleased. "Are you for real?" She darts a glance up at Logan, who is goofing off with Colby, tossing a baguette back and forth like it's a football.

"Totally." I elbow her in the ribs. "I can't believe you're so oblivious. Colby's helped him plan this whole thing, because Logan wanted to do something special for you."

"Um, I don't think Logan is the only one he did it for."

"What do you mean?"

Kylie points over at the guys. "And I don't think I'm the only oblivious one either."

I see that the boys have unpacked everything, but not into one long feast. Instead, Logan has set up his picnic basket on one end of the compartment, and Colby is at the other, waving me over with a big smile on his face.

And in that moment, I get it. It all makes sense—the funny feeling in my stomach, why Colby was so nervous every time he talked about this, why he sometimes acted all strange around me, what he meant about asking me what someone should do when they like someone else. It all clicks into place. Colby's not into Kylie. He's into *me*. Colby and . . . me. Me and Colby. My stomach does that odd twisty thing again, and I feel my cheeks grow warm. Colby likes me? Like, *like* likes me?

I walk over toward him as he pours me a little plastic cup of sparkling cider. He has a nervous, shy smile on his face. Colby, who's become one of my best friends. Colby, who looks super cute with his floppy hair and his nice eyes. Colby, who I just maybe might feel the same way about.

"So," he says nervously. "I've brought all your favorites from the different places we've been. "Florence," he says, producing a little box of cheese pizza and an ice-pack-wrapped dish of vanilla gelato. "Paris." He pulls out a thermos of hot chocolate and buttery croissants. "And, of course, London." Chips, which are really fries, and the same tin of biscuits we got back at Harrods.

I can't believe that he's gone to all this trouble. None of the food is gross. Or scary. I can't believe he's paid this close attention to me. I glance up and see he's watching me.

"Wow," I say, and then immediately feel stupid. "I mean, this is really cool, Colby. Thank you."

"I'm glad you like it," he says happily, fixing up a plate to serve me. "Bon appétit."

We munch our food while the London Eye slowly crawls toward the top, where we can look out into the pink-streaked beginning of a sunset. All of London sprawls below us, a bustling city full of people going about their ordinary business on an ordinary day, unaware of the extraordinary events unfolding in a glassed-in compartment far above them. "I'm never going to forget this," I say.

"I hope not," Colby says meaningfully, and I look back over at him. He's leaning forward, half eagerly, half nervously, and he clears his throat. "Someone I admire very much said once that if you like someone, you should just go ahead and tell them. I think it's good advice."

I hold my breath. I know he's talking about what I

said. I know he's trying to tell me he likes me, and I have absolutely no idea what to say back. In all the times I've imagined this kind of moment, I've always thought that I'd know what to say. That I'd be smooth and witty and cool, but all I feel is sweaty-palm awkward.

"I once heard her tell her dad that we were just friends," Colby continues. "But I'm kind of hoping we might be more than that." He takes a deep breath. "So, Christa, what do you think?"

"Um," I say eloquently, scrambling to think of what a normal person might say, but normality has abandoned me. I'm stuck with plain old me, and so I go with the truth. "I like you, too, Colby. Not *just* as a friend."

"Really?" He smiles at me, that slow half smile, the one I've come to know so well. The one that is absolutely gorgeous. He scoots a bit closer so we're sitting next to each other, side by side, facing the breathtaking view. All over London, lights in the city are twinkling on, glimmering little spots in the darkening sky. Ordinary house lights and streetlamps brighten up the buildings, red and green streaks paint the facade of Big Ben, and the Tower of London itself has red spotlights shadowing its turrets. Far below us the white glow of the Frostival shines brightly around the skating rink.

"Do you think," Colby begins, and he sounds nervous, "maybe, could I kiss you?"

I lean my shoulder into his, wanting to pause this moment. Okay, I admit I've never been kissed. Sure, I've imagined it a million times, studied the way the girls and boys kiss in my favorite movies, wondered what it would be like when it happened to me. And really, even if I had planned it out as much as my usual tree-decorating diagrams, I couldn't have picked a more perfect moment.

"I'd like that," I say, holding my breath a little as he leans in closer. I close my eyes, and his lips touch mine, sending little flares of electricity all through me. It's over all too soon, and I inch closer. "Maybe we should try that again," I say with a grin. "You know, for extra practice."

He laughs and scoots closer, sending those same warm sparks from my head to my toes. I cannot believe this is really happening. But then, before we have our second kiss, it all grinds to a halt. Like, literally. Our compartment jolts to a stop with a lurch that can't be normal, and fluorescent lights pop on above us with a bright glare that blots out the dreamlike landscape around us. The mood is broken.

"What's going on?" Kylie asks from the other side, and I twist around to look at them. I'd completely forgotten that they're there. She and Logan are sitting awfully close

together, and Logan's doing some cheesy thumbs-up gesture to Colby, which I guess means things are going well
on their side of the compartment, too.

A beeping sound breaks the stillness as a voice comes
through the overhead intercom. "We are experiencing
technical difficulties," a woman says in a crisp British
accent. "Please stay calm and don't panic. Repair crews are
working on the problem, and it should be fixed shortly. I
repeat, please stay calm, and wait for further updates." The
voice bleeps off, taking with it the fluorescent emergency
lights and the last vestiges of our perfect moment.

I dart a scared look over at Colby, feeling an animal-
like wave of panic grip me. That whole thing I said earlier
about not worrying? I take it back. I'm worried. It is so
not cool to hear that the machine that's got you dangling
hundreds of feet in the air is having technical problems.

"Chris?" Colby asks, reaching for my hand. "It's going
to be okay." He squeezes my hand, and I grip his back.
Hard. I hope he's right.

"Well," Logan says, seemingly unperturbed. "That's
weird. I wonder how long we're going to be stuck up here."

"Who cares?" Kylie laughs. "It's not like we have something better to do. Tonight's a free night, remember?"

Kylie's words remind me that I *do* have something else

I need to do, even if it isn't better. "But I'm supposed to see the play!" I gasp, feeling my panic ratchet up a notch.

Kylie shrugs. "For, what, like the ten millionth time? They won't miss us."

Logan chuckles. "Yeah, I could practically be an understudy I know the lines so well." He starts acting out what must be one of the scenes in the play, and Kylie joins in.

Even Colby joins in, and I realize that they've not just seen the show back in Paris when it was on the itinerary but multiple times. Probably during their free time. I bet I'm the only one who hasn't. I'm the only kid who has totally bailed on their parent, and I think, with a sinking feeling in my stomach, the only one who's about to majorly screw up again. I look at my phone. It's four thirty. Unless the London Eye crew whips this thing back into shape in the next few minutes, we're not going to meet up with the rest of the group on time.

No one else seems to be bothered by it.

"I'll text Miles," Logan says. "So he and Madison know what happened."

"Good idea," Kylie says. She pulls out her own phone and begins to take a video. "At least we've got a good view while we wait."

But the view that once felt so beautiful now feels

overwhelming. My knees tingle as I think of how very far down the ground actually is. I look at my phone and think about texting Mom. But what am I going to say that isn't going to sound like another lame excuse for ditching her play? I turn the power off, hoping that it won't matter anyway, and I'll still be able to make it to the performance.

"Try a slow breath," Colby says, gently putting an arm around my shoulder and leaning my head against his. "In and out, to help calm down."

I do as he suggests, willing my body to relax, to not cry, to not ruin what was up until a few minutes ago the best night of my life.

"How about some water?" Colby asks, handing me a bottle, and I take it gratefully.

"Do you have your map?" I think of how Colby's coping strategy helped me make it through the Chunnel. "We never finished planning out our trip."

"You bet," he says, reaching into his jacket pocket and pulling out the crumpled paper. "Where were we?"

24

COLBY AND I PLAN THREE different trips around the world when the intercom voice comes on again.

"The repairmen are nearly finished," the woman says, in a little bit of a less-calm voice this time. "We hope to have you down within the hour, and offer our sincerest apologies for the delay. Thank you for your patience."

I give a helpless laugh. Like we've had any choice. It's after ten o'clock. We've not only planned world tours, we've finished all our picnic food, told jokes, replayed moments from our trip, imitated M&M in their worst moments, and now we're all just plain tired. Even Kylie has lost some of her enthusiasm. The play is over by now, and my panic over being stuck at the top of the London Eye has melted into constant worry over how upset Mom is going to be, until even that has been dwarfed by the fact that I really, really need to pee.

Finally, the compartment lurches forward with a groaning noise, and Logan cheers, doing a one-handed flip in the center of the compartment to celebrate.

"Okay, guys, everybody scrunch together for a selfie," Kylie says, directing us to squeeze into a lump on the bench. "So we can remember this moment forever."

"How could we ever forget it?" I start to giggle, relief flooding my body at the fact that we're actually going to be on the ground soon. "It's unbelievable. Who gets stuck in the Chunnel *and* on the London Eye?"

"Us," Colby says, laughing. "Only us." We're all a bit giddy, worn out by the waiting and the emotional roller coaster of the past hours. I've gone from ordinary girl having a horrible day to magical moment; from never-been-kissed to kissed; from just me, Christa Vasile, to (maybe?) somebody's girlfriend. But none of those things has prepared me for what we find when we get off the London Eye.

Reporters are everywhere, camera bulbs flashing in our faces like we're celebrities. Somebody shoves a microphone in front of us. "What was it like to be stuck on the London Eye for six hours?" a man asks. "How did you cope?"

Kylie is the first to answer. "It was an adventure," she says, tugging Logan forward by the elbow. "We had fun."

The reporter turns to face a camera, where he's making a live update. "An adventure, ladies and gentlemen," he says in his perfect accent. "There you have it."

"Whoa," I say to Colby. "I guess this is a big deal or something."

"No kidding." He points at an ambulance parked a little way away and a first-aid tent set up nearby. EMTs are there handing out water bottles and checking one lady's blood pressure.

"Wow," I say. "I never thought about how lucky we were to have all that food." I'm delighted to see that next to the first-aid tent is a little row of Porta-Potties, and we all beeline over there. I guess I'm not the only one who's been dying for a bathroom break.

After we come out, there's a police officer standing by with a form we're supposed to fill out. He explains that they need a way to get in touch with people in case of a lawsuit.

"This is such a bigger deal than I thought it would be," Kylie says as we sit on folding chairs to complete the paperwork.

"Totally." I speedily fill out the form. Now that we're down on the ground again, I'm back to reality. All the feelings have returned—not just the good swoony Colby ones, but also the ones from this morning and the big fiasco with my parents. At this point, all I want to do is get back to the hotel. Mom's going to think I've blown her off again, and I really, really don't want things to get worse between us.

First there are more hoops to jump through. An EMT looks us over, taking our temperature and blood pressure before making us fill out another form. Then a representative from the London Eye offers us a formal apology and hands us her business card. Finally, we're through the gauntlet. The area around the entrance to the London Eye is roped off, with only emergency personnel and reporters allowed inside. Now I notice that there's a whole crowd of other people pushing up against a makeshift barricade, trying to get closer, and right in the front row is Mom, waving her red scarf like a flag in the air.

"Christa!" she calls over the others. "Over here!"

"Ohmigosh, Mom!" I shout, running toward her. I'm half expecting her to still be upset with me, but as soon as I'm within arm's reach she grabs me and squeezes me so tight. When she pulls away, I can see that she's been crying, her stage makeup a smudged ruin all over her face.

"Thank God you're okay!" She crushes me in another hug, and I can barely squeak out any words.

"I'm fine, Mom," I say, and I realize my half laugh is also a half cry as all the emotions finally catch up with me. "I'm so sorry I missed your play. I wanted to go tonight, I really did."

"Oh, Christa," Mom says. "I wasn't even there. As soon as Nic told me what had happened, I left the theater. The London Eye people wouldn't tell us anything, and I've been going crazy down here wondering what it was like for you stuck all the way up there. I tried texting you, but I guess none of them went through." She smooths my hair back from my face. "I'm so glad you're all right."

I know she's talking about my anxiety, and I tell her it was okay. "Colby helped me through it," I say, and she pulls him in for a quick hug.

"Thank God for you, Colby." She gives him a watery smile. "Your dad is right over there."

"Really?" Colby sounds surprised. "But what about the final performance?"

"We canceled it. You think any of us could do our jobs when our kids were stuck hundreds of feet above the Thames?" She points behind her, and I see that Todd is also here, as well as Logan's mom. Beyond them, Madison and Miles are huddled on a bench next to Sasha and Owen and their parents. Nic, who is talking animatedly into his cell, spots Colby then, and drops his phone back into his pocket.

"Dad!" Colby hurries over to him, leaving Mom and me alone.

Mom rummages in her bag for a tissue and wipes fruitlessly at her eyes. "I'm so sorry about this morning, hon. While you were stuck up there all I could think about was how I said such awful things to you and how horrible it would be if—"

"Mom," I cut her off. "I said a lot of stuff I didn't mean this morning."

"Me, too, honey. Me, too. No matter how complicated it gets, always remember that I love you."

"I love you, Mom." I busy myself with a tissue, since apparently I'm about to get all teary. All we need to make this the ultimate happy reunion moment is some sappy music or a slideshow of family photos, or—a familiar voice is calling my name.

"Dad?"

Mom holds up her cell phone. There's Dad, his face creased with worry.

"I've been so worried about you!" he says as we all gasp out apologies and explanations and relieved laughs.

Dad's face peers through the cell screen. "Are you okay, honey?"

"More than okay," I say truthfully.

"I wish I could have been there," Dad says. "I wish we

had done this differently. That we had figured out a way for us all to be together for this first Christmas after the divorce." He runs his hands through his uncombed hair. "You were right, Chris. Things have changed. A lot. And it's hard."

"I know," I say. "You were right, too, though. Things might be different, but that doesn't mean they have to be terrible." Thank you, Kylie, for that one. I look up at Mom. "Besides. It's okay to try new things. Maybe Christmas in Europe will become our new thing, right, Mom?"

Mom squishes me into another bear hug. I look over and see that my friends are having similar sappy moments with their parents. Colby catches my gaze, and I give him a little wave.

"So Colby was with you, huh?" Dad's voice says. "Your *friend*, right?"

"Yeah," I say slowly. "And maybe something a little bit more."

"Oh, really?" Mom leans in close. "We *do* have some catching up to do."

"See?" Dad says. "The unexpected *can* lead you someplace you were always meant to go."

"Oh, Dad, come *on*." As Mom and I walk to join the others after saying good-bye to Dad, I realize that he was right. Everything about this trip has been different than I expected it to be, but looking around the group, I see how it's taken me to some really great places after all.

Miles knows about a breakfast restaurant that's open late. He and Madison lead all of us—Todd and Kylie, Colby and Nic, Sasha and Owen and Logan and all the parents, and me and my mom—over to Ossie's Cafe. On the way, Mom asks me how the last dare went.

"I didn't even look at it," I confess, thinking of the rumpled envelope back on the hotel bed.

"There's still time to finish the scavenger hunt," Mom says with a grin. "The twelfth dare is to find the beauty that's present all around you."

"Oh, that's an easy one," I say, grinning at Mom. "Every moment is a gift." I link arms with her. "Especially this one."

Up ahead, Kylie and Todd start singing "Silent Night," and Mom begins to sing along. Hearing her voice, I feel all warm inside. I've never gone Christmas caroling with Mom. Maybe things can't be like they were before, but we can start making space for new traditions, traditions that could lead us to unexpectedly good places.

I join in, and soon we're all caroling quietly on the late-night London streets. When we reach the restaurant, we're pretty much the only people there, so the staff squishes together the smaller tables to make one super-long table that we all crowd around. I'm happy when Colby slides into the seat next to me. He points to his watch.

"It's midnight." Then he looks at me with his perfect eyes. "Merry Christmas, Christa."

"Merry Christmas." I blush, thinking about the way his lips felt on mine and how nice it was to lean up against him. For once, I'm not worried about what might happen. I'm excited to find out what comes next.

The waiter makes his way around, handing out menus to everyone. I hold mine in front of me, but I'm not actually reading it. Instead, I'm looking past it to our group around the table: my new friends, my newish relationship with Mom. I think about how the dares have sort of brought me all of this. They gave me experiences that forced me to be brave and try challenging things. They taught me that change doesn't always mean something bad. They also brought me people—new friends and the beginnings of a mended relationship with my parents and, perhaps most unexpected of all, Colby. I think of all this, and I link my hand with Colby's.

When the waiter comes to take my order, I shut my menu without even looking at it. I hand it back to him and take a deep breath. "Why don't you surprise me?"

ACKNOWLEDGMENTS

I am grateful and humbled to see this fifth (FIFTH!) book go to print, and I especially appreciate all those who work behind the scenes to transform this document into the beautiful printed book you hold in your hands:

Laura Langlie: Thank you for your optimism, editorial input, and advocacy. You are an outstanding agent, and I am so happy that we get to work together.

Claudia Gabel and Rebecca Aronson: I count it a privilege to have had the opportunity to bring this book idea to life. It's been a pleasure working with both of you, and your editorial notes, personal vulnerability, and creative input have been instrumental in the story and have also helped me grow as a writer. Many thanks to both of you.

The team at HarperCollins: I wish I knew all of your names and faces, because then I could personally tell you how blown away I always am by your creative ideas for book covers, fonts, page layouts, and all those many details that make each book special. Thank you!

Melissa Neikirk: Thank you, dear friend, for sharing your story with me. I'm so honored that I get to know you! I so appreciate you and Josh brainstorming with me early on about the book's opening and themes.

Jeremiah Webster: Your editorial notes and kind thoughts on the first chapters were motivating and timely. You and Kristin, and L&M, are so dear to us. Thank you both for being my friends in this writing endeavor and in so much else. You all are such a delightful gift.

Casey Walton: Besides being a dear friend whose encouragement is much appreciated, you have contributed enormously to the research behind the European locations and the dynamic of traveling with a student group. Thank you for sharing your tour director experience and brilliant ideas for the dares and for being such a good friend to me (and all of us) over the years. I'm so glad you agreed to cat-sit so many moons ago.

Griffin, Elijah, Ransom, and Beatrix: What can I say? I love you all so much and can hardly believe I get to spend my days with you. I am so grateful for all of our shared memories and little family jokes and the stories you tell me and your silly dances and all the million and one things that make each of you as individuals and all of you together so incredibly amazing. It is so fun to get to be your mom. Thank you for every minute of it.

Aaron: I'm crazy about you. For this book in particular, I'll just include here how deeply thankful I am for your gentleness with all of my neuroses. :) Nineteen-year-old you and me had no real idea what we were doing, but thank God He did. I'm so glad to be yours.

And to the Lord, the giver of all good gifts, including the Greatest Christmas Gift, Jesus Himself: I love you so much. You are everything to me. Thank you.